75p

D0264717

Stories from Ovid

BY

MARTIN MURPHY

Illustrated by
June Barber

OXFORD UNIVERSITY PRESS
1971

Oxford University Press, Ely House, London W.1

GLASGOW NEW YORK TORONTO MELBOURNE WELLINGTON
CAPE TOWN SALISBURY IBADAN NAIROBI DAR ES SALAAM LUSAKA ADDIS ABABA
BOMBAY CALCUTTA MADRAS KARACHI LAHORE DACCA
KUALA LUMPUR SINGAPORE HONG KONG TOKYO

PHOTOSET BY BAS PRINTERS LTD., WALLOP, HAMPSHIRE
AND PRINTED LITHOGRAPHICALLY IN GREAT BRITAIN
AT THE UNIVERSITY PRESS, OXFORD
BY VIVIAN RIDLER
PRINTER TO THE UNIVERSITY

Contents

List of Illustrations

Introduction

The stories that follow are all taken from a long epic poem by the Roman poet Ovid (43 B.C.–A.D. 17) called the *Metamorphoses*—a Greek word which means 'changes of shape'. Ovid took his stories mainly from Greek mythology: they are of many different kinds but they all include some sort of transformation, usually the transformation of a man or woman into an animal or a natural object. Perhaps the best known of these transformation stories is the myth of Circe, which is to be found in Homer's *Odyssey*. Circe was the sorceress who with her magic wand turned Odysseus' men into pigs, but was then outwitted by the hero who resisted her spell because he was armed with a powerful herb given him as protection by the god Hermes. There were many other such stories in ancient folklore. Primitive people, like children, were quick to see human features in the odd shapes of rocks, trees and animals and then they invented stories to explain these resemblances. We have only to think of the Giant's Causeway in Northern Ireland, of the Old Man of Hoy in the Orkneys or of the Needles off the Isle of Wight, to see how our own ancestors explained away curious features of the landscape in human terms: it would be easy to invent stories about the origin of all three of these places. The Greeks were no exception to this rule: the story of Arachne, for instance, starts from observation that the spider acts like a weaver at the loom; from there it is a short step to saying that the spider was originally a human weaver who was changed into her present shape as a punishment for pride.

Primitive people were naturally religious, that is to say they had a deep reverence and respect for the unseen powers in the world about them. They imagined that each tree, each stream had its own protecting divine spirit, for the whole world was full of gods—hidden forces that must not be offended. Some philosophers like the Greek Pythagoras believed that the souls or spirits of all living things were really part of the one divine spirit, with which they were finally united after passing through several different existences. Someone who is a man in his present existence may have to be a hedgehog or a squirrel in his next. These beliefs encouraged a deep respect for all forms of life and a conviction that though the world seems to be continually changing there is an unchanging unity beneath it all. Ovid was certainly familiar with these ideas and even mentions Pythagoras in his poem. His own style of writing is brilliantly suited to this subject of change. Just as the characters change their shapes, so the scene continually changes from one place to another with each new story or within the one story, and the mood also changes from serious to comic, from the savage to the tender. In the variety of his style, Ovid has as many different disguises as Proteus, one of the characters of the *Metamorphoses*, the old man of the sea who could change into any shape at will.

No one nation has ever invented such a wide variety of beautiful stories or myths as the Greeks. In writing his poem, then, Ovid had a rich store of Greek legend on which to draw, and the *Metamorphoses* is perhaps the best collection of these stories that has ever been made. Someone has called it 'the Who's Who of ancient mythology'. However, Ovid treated these ancient stories in what was, at the time, a modern way. The world of Rome into which Ovid was born (in 43 B.C.) was as far removed from the world of Greek legend as our modern world is removed from King Arthur's Avalon. What gives the *Metamorphoses* its spice and wit is that Ovid treats the gods and men of legend as if they were modern Romans. In the 'Io' story for instance, the mighty Jupiter behaves like any ordinary henpecked husband, and elsewhere when Mercury flies down to earth to court a mortal girl Ovid describes how he combs his hair and arranges his tunic just like a young Roman dandy before an evening out with his girl friend. It was nothing new of course to represent the gods as being jealous or weak or just plain silly. Educated Greeks and Romans did not regard this as shocking because they knew that the gods of mythology, the gods described by Homer and the poets, belonged to the world of the imagination, not to the world of fact. Still, at the time when Ovid was writing, Augustus, the new head of the Roman state, was trying to revive the worship of the 'official' gods such as Jupiter and Juno and so he cannot have been pleased at the irreverent way in which their names were treated in the *Metamorphoses*. Ovid takes a particular delight in contrasting the dignity of the gods' position with the highly undignified situations in which their love affairs

6

involve them. From this we may guess that Ovid himself had little respect for the pompous or the self-important, and perhaps this is another reason why he became unpopular with the official authorities.

Not only are the characters of the *Metamorphoses* treated in a 'modern' way, but there are many direct references to the everyday life of Ovid's Rome. For instance, when Cadmus sows the dragon's teeth and armed warriors spring up out of the soil, Ovid compares the sight to what happens at the theatre when the curtain is raised (Roman curtains were not dropped, but drawn up from a roll at the bottom) and the painted figures on it gradually rise into view, beginning with their heads. Or again when Pyramus stabs himself over the body of his beloved Thisbe, we are told that the blood spurted up like the jet of water from a burst pipe in the Roman streets! These details are what we would call anachronisms, but they bring a vivid liveliness to the story-telling. The most striking details are about city life, because although Ovid was born in a country town in central Italy he was happiest when at Rome. This was unusual for a Roman poet. Others, such as Horace and Virgil, were always saying how they longed to be away from the bustling streets and return to the peace of the countryside: they praised the good old days when the Romans were content with simple pleasures and stayed at home on the farm. But Ovid tells us frankly that he preferred the advantages of modern life and was not ashamed to enjoy its more sophisticated pleasures. This cannot have made him popular with Augustus who was trying to reform the morals of smart society. Augustus wanted his poets to make people conscious of the grandeur and dignity of Rome and to put his ideals into noble words. Virgil and Horace succeeded in doing this magnificently but Ovid was not at his best when writing 'official' poetry and the weakest parts of the *Metamorphoses*, for instance, are those in which he tries to do just this. The last of the *Metamorphoses*, describing the transformation of Julius Caesar into an immortal star, was clearly written to please Augustus but it sounds lifeless.

Eventually, for reasons which are not known, Ovid fell foul of Augustus and in A.D. 8 he was banished to the remote Black Sea coast of what is now Rumania. There he spent the last eleven years of his life among the 'barbarians', as he called them—pining for the city and the friends he loved so much. Augustus could hardly have devised a more cruel punishment for a man who was so fond of the pleasures of society. Ovid died, still exiled, in A.D. 17, three years after Augustus himself.

Ovid had the advantage of being a supreme story teller. Though each of the fifteen books of the *Metamorphoses* contains many different stories, he links them so craftily that we hardly notice the joins. The pace of the story is never allowed to flag but carries the reader forward. We have already mentioned Ovid's humour, but only second to this is his tenderness and humanity. Nowhere in Roman poetry is the love of husband and wife so tenderly described as, for instance, in the story of Ceyx and Alcyone. There is a delicate pity too for those who cannot express their feelings: we have only to think of Actaeon, turned into a stag, turning his eyes pleadingly towards his own hounds who are about to tear him to pieces. English people are accustomed to the idea of feeling pity for dumb animals, but it is rare to find this feeling in a Roman.

But the most remarkable of Ovid's qualities and the one which accounts for his great popularity with poets and artists ever since is his ability to describe a scene so vividly that we can picture every detail before our eyes. Above all he excels in the description of light and of water: think for instance of the pool where Arethusa goes to bathe on a warm summer afternoon, the water so still 'that you could count every pebble on the river-bed'. No poet has ever been so accomplished a painter with words, and that is why the Italian painters of the Renaissance returned again and again to the *Metamorphoses* for their scenes and subjects.

Besides being able to describe scenes, Ovid can also enter into the minds of his characters and describe their feelings from within. He has a particular understanding of children and women. Read, for instance, his account of young Phaethon, so eager to tackle a man's job and so determined to get what he wants, in spite of his father's pleadings. Ovid's understanding of women is even more profound and he is particularly fond of describing inner conflicts when one of his heroines is debating what course of action to take. Ovid, like all young Romans of his class had been well drilled in the art of debate or 'rhetoric', as it was called, and sometimes his characters sound uncommonly like debaters, anxious to score points off their opponents.

8

Nowadays we find this 'rhetoric' rather artificial but it was much admired in literary circles at Rome. A good example of such rhetoric is the passage in which Medea debates with herself whether or not to help Jason against her father: as she puts the 'pros' and 'cons' to herself, her mind changes with each new argument on either side.

Ovid's brilliant fables have had a great influence on European literature of all periods. His vivid, sensuous descriptions of legendary scenes were especially popular in the Middle Ages, though medieval writers always tried to interpret the stories of the *Metamorphoses* as 'allegories'—containing some moral lesson. They were quick to discover similarities between Ovid's characters and the characters of the Bible: thus Deucalion and Pyrrha were compared with Noah and his wife, and Phaethon's fall was compared with Lucifer's. The painters and poets of the Renaissance, however, were not ashamed to enjoy the *Metamorphoses* for their own sake, and Elizabethan schoolboys (like William Shakespeare at Stratford on Avon) were steeped in the study of Ovid. The first English translation of the *Metamorphoses* (or rather an English translation of a French translation!) was written in 1480 by William Caxton, the printer, but by far the best version was that of William Golding (1567). In Golding's version Ovid's characters are transformed into jolly English country people who talk and act with tremendous gusto and even lapse into broad Somerset dialect. Golding's style is very far removed from Ovid's smooth and polished verse but it is all done with great enjoyment and has twice as much life as many more accurate translations. Shakespeare almost certainly knew his Golding, but Milton had no need of translations: he was a scholar who even wrote Latin poetry of his own, and we know that the *Metamorphoses* was his favourite book in youth and in old age. Marlowe, Spenser, Dryden—these are only a few of the many English poets whose imagination was fed on the beauty of the *Metamorphoses*. It was only in the nineteenth century that Ovid fell out of favour in England, perhaps because he was thought to be too frivolous. Nowadays we can value Ovid not only for his own sake, as a superlative artist, but because he shows us that behind the façade of Augustan Rome, behind all the military glory and moral earnestness and public parade, there was still a place for tenderness and humour and the appreciation of beauty.

1. Lycaon

Many of the Greek myths look back longingly to a Golden Age in the distant past when the world was free of war and suffering and cruelty, and they use the same words to describe this past age as the Jewish prophets like Isaiah used to describe a future age, when God would give his people rest and peace.

There are other ways in which this story reminds us of the Bible. The book of Genesis tells us that Adam, the father of the human race, was originally placed by God in a paradise of pleasure but then lost his happiness by disobeying God's command. In the Greek story as told here by Ovid, man again loses his happiness, but the loss is not so sudden: there is a gradual decline from the Golden to the Iron Age. Both stories tell us about the longing for goodness and innocence which is always felt by the human heart.

Ovid describes the metamorphosis of Lycaon so naturally that we have no time to think it odd. Lycaon behaved so wolfishly as a man that when he is turned into a real wolf it seems somehow appropriate. In the folklore of other nations there are similar stories of 'werewolves', and in fact there have been real cases of people imagining themselves to be wolves.

With the story of the Flood we return to a theme which is again familiar to us from the Bible and its account of Noah. Such stories are to be found all over the world, and in Babylonia, at least, the story has been proved true because there archaeologists have discovered certain traces of a massive deluge which swamped the land. Ovid is chiefly interested in the odd contrasts produced by the flood.

The first age of man was the Golden Age, when the peoples of the world lived in peace and the earth flowed with milk and honey. Then followed the Silver Age, when the world passed from the rule of Saturn to that of his son Jupiter. It was Jupiter who divided the year into four seasons, so that for the first time men felt the hot blast of summer and the icy chill of winter, and had to take shelter in caves or build huts from branches and bark. After that came the Bronze Age, when men were fiercer and more eager to make war but had not yet become wicked. It was the Iron Age, the last age of man, which turned the world to evil and put goodness and truth to flight. People thought only of money and war, and sons turned against fathers, mothers against daughters in treachery and greed. Even heaven itself was not safe. For the giants tried to climb up to heaven by uprooting the mountains and piling them one on top of another. But Jupiter smashed the towering mass with his thunderbolt so that it toppled down, burying and crushing all below in a mighty avalanche. The blood of the giants soaked into the earth, but the earth did not want all trace of her children to be destroyed, and breathed new life into the warm blood. So there arose a new race of men, the children of blood, as violent and cruel as their fathers.

The crimes of the children of blood came to the ears of Jupiter, up on Mount Olympus, and he decided to go down to earth to see for himself. As he wandered through the land of Greece he came at nightfall to the house of Lycaon, the king of Arcady, and there he asked for shelter. He told everyone he was a god but when the ordinary people bowed down and adored him, Lycaon only laughed. 'We'll soon see whether he is really a god,' he said. That night he tried to kill Jupiter when he was asleep, and when this did not succeed he turned to a more dreadful crime yet. There were hostages in his palace from the land of the Molossians, and calling one of them he slit his throat and cut up his flesh, boiling some of it and roasting the rest, with the intention of serving the foul dish for Jupiter to eat. But as soon as he placed it on the table, his house burst into flames and Lycaon fled in terror. He tried to cry out but instead of a cry came a dreadful howl; he foamed at the mouth and in his blood-lust fell not upon men but upon sheep. His clothes turned into shaggy hair, his arms into paws: he was a wolf. So did Jupiter punish Lycaon, but not only Lycaon had sinned: madness and evil stalked throughout the whole world, and the whole world had to be punished.

Jupiter called a meeting of all the gods in the courtyard of his palace on Mount Olympus. 'The whole race of men must be destroyed', he told them, 'for the world will never be safe from their wickedness while they live.' When the gods and goddesses heard of Lycaon's dreadful crime, they raised a great shout of indignation that echoed round the hall, and with one accord they approved Jupiter's decision. Yet secretly some of them were anxious and wondered what the world would be like if it were empty of men. There would be no one to place offerings at their altars and shrines, and wild beasts would roam freely through the forests unchecked. Jupiter soothed

their fears. 'Do not be alarmed,' he said. 'Before long I will create a new race of men quite unlike the old.'

At first Jupiter intended to set the earth ablaze by showering it with his thunderbolts, but he was afraid that the whole vault of heaven might catch fire and the entire universe be destroyed. So he decided instead to drown mankind beneath the waves and deluged them from above with his rainclouds which burst in an endless downpour, flattening the crops. Locking up all the other winds in a prison cave, he surrendered the sky to the South Wind. On soaking wings the South Wind flew through the dark air, his plumes heavy with rain and his long white hair dripping with moisture. Neptune, too, came to his brother's aid, and calling the rivers together he commanded them to let loose their waters in full flood. Across the wide plains the rivers raced, sweeping houses and cattle and trees in their path, the torrent rising higher and higher till the whole earth was one surging lake. Men took to boats and sailed above the fields they had only recently ploughed. Fish were caught as they swam among the topmost branches of trees. Ugly seals now wallowed where frisky goats had once cropped the grass. Wolves swam among flocks of sheep and even lions and tigers took to the waves. Wandering birds flew endlessly over the water, looking in vain for some dry land until at last they sank down in exhaustion, their wings soaked by the waves. Even the mountain peaks were washed by the tide. The greater part of mankind was drowned and those who survived perished of starvation.

2. Deucalion and Pyrrha

Deucalion and Pyrrha are just like Noah and his wife: because of their faithfulness they are saved from the flood that destroys the rest of mankind and then they bring a new race of men into being. In describing the metamorphosis of stones into human shapes, Ovid plays on the fact that some stones like marble are veined in a way similar to the human body. Variations of this story are to be found all over the world, even in South America. According to the version told by some tribes in British Guiana and along the Orinoco river, the two survivors of the flood threw coconuts, not stones, over their shoulders!

As the waters of the Flood swelled up over the earth they carried with them a small boat containing two survivors of the human race, Deucalion and Pyrrha. This gentle and god-fearing pair had been spared from destruction by Jupiter and marked out as founders of a new family of men. Their boat drifted on the dark torrent until at last it stuck fast on the summit of Mount Parnassus, where the topmost peak rose above the water, and there on the roof of the world Deucalion and Pyrrha stepped out and offered sacrifice to the gods. Seeing that the whole world was now covered by a vast shimmering lake and that these two were all that was left of the whole human race, Jupiter scattered the thick thunder clouds and once more opened up the sky to earth and earth to sky, bathing the world in brilliant sunshine. Neptune, too, calmed the sea and laid down his trident.

At his command, sea-green Triton emerged waist-high from the
waves, his shoulders crusted with shell-fish and hair bedewed with
brine; he blew upon his whorled sea-shell horn, as signal for the waters
to withdraw. As the last notes echoed through the stillness, the waves

15

began to sink. Soon the sea-shore reappeared, rivers returned to their beds as the hills and fields emerged, and by the time the day drew to its close even the tree-tops were uncovered, their leaves now caked in mud. In the darkening light Deucalion gazed in awe at the empty and desolate world uncovered beneath him and wept. 'Pyrrha,' he said,

16

'we are all that is left of mankind. We have no one but each other, and who knows when the rains will come again to drown us in another flood? If only I could breathe life into the earth and create new men from the clay as my father did—men modelled on ourselves!' Then they decided to make their prayer to the gods. First they sprinkled their heads and their clothes with holy water drawn from the stream of Cephisus, and then they approached the temple of Themis, the goddess of justice. Her shrine was still covered with seaweed and moss from the flood, the stones were yellow and no fires burned in the cold, damp hearth. The lonely pair stretched themselves out on the altar steps and kissed the cold marble. 'Themis', they prayed, 'if you have any mercy, if the gods can be softened by prayer, tell us how to restore mankind; bring help to our drowned world.' Moved with pity the goddess answered them with words of mystery: 'Leave this temple, veil your heads,' she said; 'loosen your robes and then throw the bones of the great mother over your shoulder.' Pyrrha was horrified and at first refused to obey the goddess. 'My mother's bones?' she cried. 'How can I disturb my mother's ghost?' But Deucalion pondered the goddess' words deeply in his heart, and tried to soothe his wife's fears. 'The gods could not tell us to do anything wrong,' he said. 'No, I see it now. The great mother, that is the earth, and by her "bones" are meant the stones that lie on the earth's body. It is stones we must throw over our shoulders.' Pyrrha was almost convinced, and though she and Deucalion could hardly believe their hopes, they thought there would be no harm in trying. So they went away, and after veiling their heads and loosening their robes they threw stones behind them as the goddess had commanded.

Almost at once, they say, the stones began to lose their hardness and stiffness and gradually became soft and shapely. Slowly they appeared to take on human outlines, like blocks of marble which a sculptor has left unfinished. The damp parts, where the clay was still moist, were transformed into flesh, while the hard and solid parts became bone, and blood coursed through the veins of stone. So by the power of the gods Deucalion's stones were changed to men and Pyrrha's to women. Mankind was re-created, a new and hardy race.

3. Apollo and Daphne

Of all Ovid's metamorphosis stories this has always been the most popular with artists and sculptors. A famous statue, now in the Vatican Museum, by the eighteenth-century Italian artist Bernini appears as a frontispiece. It shows Daphne at the very moment of her transformation, and every detail of the sculpture is modelled on Ovid's account. Another beautiful painting of the same scene by Pollaiuolo, a fifteenth-century Florentine painter, is now in the National Gallery, London.

The word Daphne in Greek means laurel, and perhaps this story was invented to explain why the laurel played such an important part in the worship of Apollo, who was the god of poetry and medicine and prophecy as well as of archery. The laurel was used to crown famous poets and musicians, as well as for medicinal purposes, and at Apollo's oracle in Delphi the prophetess used to chew the leaves in order to work herself up into a state of inspiration. In Ovid's own day at Rome, victorious generals were crowned with laurel, and the entrance to the emperor's palace at Rome on the Palatine Hill was flanked by two of the trees.

Ovid loves to cut the gods down to size and here in the description of Apollo he makes the most of the comic situation.

It was no accident that made Phoebus Apollo fall in love with Daphne. It was spiteful Cupid who arranged it, to get his revenge on the god for sneering at him. Apollo had only recently killed a monster serpent and was swaggering about, enjoying everyone's admiration, when he saw young Cupid practising with his bow and arrows. 'What is a giddy boy like you doing with a man's weapons?' he said, scornfully. 'Archery is my business, and my arrows never miss—whether I'm shooting wild beasts or my own enemies. Why, only the other day I killed that giant bloated Python with a well-aimed volley. You should have seen its size! It flattened acres and acres with its enormous belly. If I were you, I'd leave well alone, little boy! You can't compete with me, you know!' This really stung Cupid. 'Your arrows may pierce everyone else, Apollo,' he retorted, 'but mine are going to pierce *you*!' And with that he flew off, beating the air with his wings, until he landed on the shady summit of Parnassus. There from his quiver he

chose two arrows, one which arouses the fire of love and another which kills it stone dead. The former was made of gold, with a sharp, shining point and this was the one Cupid shot at Apollo, so that it penetrated deep into the marrow of his bones. The other one, blunt and lined with lead, he fired straight at Daphne. So while Apollo fell

head over heels in love, poor Daphne would not hear of the idea and ran off to the depths of the forest, living as a huntress like the goddess Diana. She had many suitors but she would have nothing to do with any of them, preferring to wander through the silent glades, all by herself. Marriage was quite out of the question. Her poor father was very upset, but whenever he suggested that it was time she was thinking of getting a husband, Daphne would blush crimson. 'Father darling,' she begged, 'please let me stay as I am! Diana's father let her stay single, so why can't you?' Her father had to agree, but it really was a shame: Daphne was such a good-looking girl. Well, you can imagine what happened when Phoebus saw her. There and then

20

he determined that Daphne was to be his wife. He caught the flame of love as quickly as the stubble in a harvested cornfield or as bracken near a wayfarer's camp-fire. He was ablaze with love for Daphne, and everything about her added fuel to the flames. While she ran off as fast as the wind, he called after her desperately: 'Daphne, stop, please! I'm your friend! Stop! Daphne! You run away from me like a lamb fleeing from a wolf, a deer from a lion or a dove from an eagle. But this is different. I'm only running after you because I love you. Oh dear oh dear! You'll trip over in a minute and scratch your tender legs on the brambles and hurt yourself—all because of me. Do be careful and run a little slower. I promise I won't cheat by catching up with you! Anyway, do you know who I am? I'm no mountain man, no uncouth shepherd. You're only running away, you silly girl, because you don't know me. I'm Jupiter's son. It is by my power that prophets tell the past, present and future. It is by my power that poets set their songs to music. No arrows shoot straighter than mine— save only Cupid's arrow which has pierced my empty heart. I invented medicine, too, and taught men how to use herbs as cures. But what good is that to me now, when no herbs can cure this love of mine?'

He would have gone on, but Daphne fled in terror leaving him gaping in mid-sentence. How beautiful she looked as she ran, with her delicate hair streaming in the wind. Young Apollo did not waste any more time with useless compliments but followed faster than ever. He was like a hunting dog that catches sight of a hare in an open field and gives chase, hot on the trail, with its straining muzzle almost reaching its prey, while the poor hare hardly knows whether it is already caught or not, and can feel its pursuer's breath hot on its back. But Apollo, swift on the wings of love, soon began to gain ground. Daphne could feel him breathing down her neck now, and her strength began to give way. She was already pale with fear and exhaustion when she suddenly caught sight of the waters of her father Peneus, the river-god. 'Father!' she cried, 'help me! If your rivers really have divine power, then take away the lovely looks which have brought me so much trouble!' Scarcely had she finished speaking when a heavy numbness began to creep over her limbs, a thin bark spread over her body, her hair sprouted into leaves, her arms grew into branches, her feet—once so swift—clung rooted to the earth,

and a waving tree-top closed over her face. She was a laurel—as lovely as ever, of course.

Laurel or not—Phoebus still loved her. As he laid his hand on the trunk he could feel Daphne's heart still fluttering beneath the fresh bark and when he put his arms round her branches he could feel them shrinking back. 'Very well, then', he cried; 'if you can't be my wife, then at least you shall be my very own tree. Your laurel wreath shall always crown my head and the heads of my poets. It will crown the heads of Roman generals, too, when they drive in triumph to the Capitol as the people sing a hymn of victory. Your trees shall stand sentry before the very palace of the emperor, flanking the wreath of oak-leaves that hangs above his gates. And since your leaves are to crown my head, the head of an immortal god, so they will never die, but keep their beauty evergreen!'

Apollo had finished. As for the laurel tree, it nodded ever so gently with its new-made branches, as if to show its approval of his words.

22

4. Io

Notice again how Ovid enjoys describing the gods as if they were ordinary people: the great Jupiter behaves just like any timid husband persecuted by a nagging wife. We are made to feel sorry for poor Io when she finds she no longer has words to express her feelings. In writing this perhaps Ovid was thinking of the pleading and piteous looks animals sometimes give us, as if they wanted to tell us their needs and sufferings.

After the Argus episode (obviously invented in order to explain the curious pattern of eyes which is to be seen in the peacock's tail), the story ends in Egypt. This is all because of a misunderstanding. It was wrongly thought in Ovid's time that Io was another name for the Egyptian goddess Isis—perhaps because Isis was always depicted with a cow's horns on her head. The religion of Isis was very popular throughout the Roman world in Ovid's day.

Io was the daughter of the river god Inachus. One day she was returning from a bathe in her father's stream when she was seen by Jupiter, who promptly fell in love with her. 'Io!' he cried out, 'don't run away. I love you. I'm not one of your common or garden gods— I'm Jupiter, lord of the thunderbolts. You should count yourself lucky, my girl.' Now, of course, while he was courting Io, Jupiter didn't want to be seen by anyone, so he hid himself and the girl in a thick, misty cloud. Meanwhile his wife Juno was looking down from the heights of Mount Olympus, where the gods live. It was a fine day and so she was surprised when she saw this cloud suddenly appearing down on the ground. She looked around for her husband but he was nowhere to be seen. 'Jupiter's up to something again', she said to herself, and at once she set off down to earth to investigate what was going on. Jupiter saw her coming and so, to hide Io, he turned her into a cow—a very pretty cow to be sure. When Juno blew the cloud away and saw the cow, she didn't know what to think, though she had a good idea of what was going on. 'Do you like my cow?' asked her husband, innocently. Juno had to agree that it was a very good-looking cow. 'Where does it come from, and who does it belong to?' she asked, as if she didn't suspect anything. Jupiter gulped. 'Oh, I

don't know', he said vaguely. 'I just found it'. Obviously he didn't
want Juno to know the truth, but Juno persisted. 'Oh do let me have
it as a present', she pleaded. Poor Jupiter was desperate. He didn't
want to let his beloved Io out of his sight, but if he refused to give
the 'cow' to his wife she might suspect that it wasn't a cow at all. In
the end his caution proved the better of his love, and Juno had her
way. She was determined that the cow should never escape and so
she placed it under the watchful care of Argus, the monster with a
hundred eyes.

Day and night Argus kept watch over Io, never letting her out of his sight. He closed two of his eyes at a time, to give a rest to all in turn, but meanwhile the other ninety-eight were open and watchful on every side. Wherever Io went, behind or in front, to right or to left, Argus was always watching. During the day-time he let his captive graze on the grass, but at sunset he shut her up and put a chain round her neck. Poor Io! With only bitter grass to eat and muddy water to drink, with only the hard ground for her bed, she was reduced to misery. She tried to stretch out her arms to beg Argus for mercy, but she found there were no arms to stretch, and when she tried to plead with him, out of her mouth came a loud mooing sound that made her jump with fright. As she grazed over the countryside she came at last to her father's stream, and when she looked down and saw her horns reflected in the water, she started back in terror. Her father Inachus and her playmates the river nymphs caught sight of her, little knowing who she was, and she followed them around seeking to be fondled and admired. Inachus took a handful of grass and when he held it out she took it and licked his hand, covering it with kisses as the tears welled up in her eyes. If only she had words to beg for help and tell him her name! But the words would not come, and all she could do was to draw her name in the dust with her hoof to show who she was. Inachus, seeing the letters in the dust, could not restrain his grief and flung his arms around his daughter's snow-white neck. 'O my daughter,' he cried, 'to think that I have searched the whole earth for you, only to find you like this! And now you cannot answer me or speak to me, save by sighs. I was looking forward to seeing you married to a fine husband, but now—now I only want to die, and yet I cannot even do that, because I am a god.' Even as he lamented, Argus of the hundred eyes drove Io away to new pastures, away from her father. As his prisoner cropped the grass he himself sat on a hill from which he could see in all directions.

But Jupiter could not bear to see Io suffering any more and calling Mercury, the messenger god, he commanded him to seek out Argus and put him to death. Mercury set out from the heights of Olympus and when he had reached the ground he laid aside his wings and his traveller's hat and went on his way as a shepherd, driving his flocks along the country by-ways and playing his pipes as he went. When

Argus saw him coming he called out 'Come and join me up here. There's good pasture for sheep and cool shade for resting'. Mercury accepted the invitation and kept Argus entranced with his conversation and his music. The music of the pipes was bewitchingly soothing and as time went by Argus became drowsier and drowsier. First one eye closed, then another, and though Argus struggled to keep awake, at last it was too much for him. When every single eye was safely shut Mercury gently touched them with his magic wand, and then, drawing his curved sword, he cut off Argus' head and threw it over the cliff of the hill. But Juno saw what had happened, and she caught the hundred eyes as they fell and set them in the tail of her favourite bird, the peacock, where they are still to be found to this day. She was furious, and to take her revenge she sent a demon to torment Io and drive her headlong over the earth. Io ran on and on until at last she reached the banks of the Nile. There, sinking down on her knees and lifting her head piteously, she begged Juno to have pity on her and bring her troubles to an end. Juno was hard to persuade, but at last she relented, and then straightway Io began to return to her former shape. The horns disappeared, her eyes and mouth grew smaller, her arms and hands returned and soon there was nothing of the cow left in her, unless you count its whiteness and beauty. Io stood up and ever so timidly—for she was out of practice—she began to speak. When she recovered, she settled down in Egypt and there, even today, she is worshipped as a goddess.

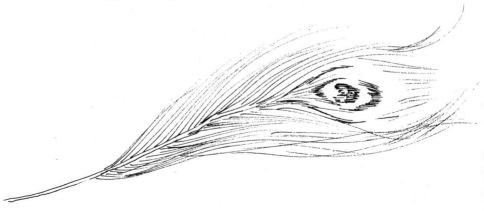

5. Phaethon

Just as the story of Deucalion and Pyrrha reflects a deep primitive fear of a world flood, so the story of Phaethon reflects man's fear of what might happen if the sun were one day to run off its course and set the world on fire. Nowadays the story would take the form not of myth but of science fiction. Ovid, as usual, never lets us forget the human feelings involved. With him we share the feelings of Phaethon: we share his boyish longing to do a man's job (what boy does not want to drive his father's car?) and then we share his horror and fear when he realizes that the job is beyond his control. When Phaethon looks down at the world dizzily spinning beneath him the effect is as realistic as in the cinema.

Sicilian coin: the sun god driving his chariot

Medieval writers, who were always quick to spot resemblances between classical legend and the Bible, identified Phaethon's fall with the fall of Lucifer. The great English poet John Milton, who learned to love Ovid as a boy at school, used his memories of the Phaethon story to great effect when he described the fall of Lucifer in his epic poem *Paradise Lost*. Shakespeare, too, was fascinated by the story. There is a reference to it, for example, in *The Two Gentlemen of Verona* (iii, 1):

> 'Why Phaethon—for thou art Merops' son—
> Wilt thou aspire to guide the heavenly car,
> And with thy daring folly burn the world?'

Phaethon, who lived with his mother Clymene, was the son of Phoebus, the sun-god. He had never seen his father, but he used to boast about him to the other boys at school. One day his friend Epaphus, who was himself the son of Jupiter, could stand it no longer. 'You're always talking so big!' he sneered. 'Phoebus isn't your father at all. You must be silly to believe everything your mother tells you!' Phaethon blushed deep red and it was all he could do to fight down his anger. Bursting with indignation and shame he went and told Clymene about the insulting taunts Epaphus had thrown at him. 'And mother,' he cried, 'what makes it worse is that I just stood there and let him say it! I just couldn't think of any way to prove him wrong. To think he could get away with it!' He put his arms round her. 'Mother', he said, 'I must have proof that Phoebus really is my father. You must help me.'

Clymene was so moved by her son's young pride, and so angered by what he had told her, that she solemnly raised her hands and lifting up her eyes towards the sun she said, 'If I am not telling you the truth, my son, if Phoebus is not your father, then may he himself take away the light from my eyes. But you are a strong and brave boy, Phaethon. It is time for you to visit your father yourself. It is not very difficult to find the land of the sunrise. Go to him. He will tell you the truth.'

Hardly had she spoken when Phaethon dashed out of the house in high spirits. He passed through his own native country of Ethiopia, through the hot lands of India, until at last, at the eastern edge of the world, climbing a steep path, he stood in front of the Palace of the Sun. Passing through doors of ivory and silver flanked by golden columns, he entered the palace but at first kept his distance from Phoebus as his eyes could not bear the brilliance of the light which shone from him. Dressed in shining robes the sun-god sat high up on a throne which flashed with emeralds, surrounded by his courtiers and attendants. Next to him were Day and Month and Year, and the Hours, placed at regular intervals. Then there were the Centuries and the four Seasons: Spring, garlanded with fresh flowers, Summer, lightly clad and covered with a wreath of barley corn, Autumn with her feet still stained by the juice of the wine-press, and icy, white-haired Winter. Young Phaethon stood stock still in amazement at the brilliant scene until at last his father spoke. 'My son', he said, 'what brings you here?' 'Father', Phaethon replied, 'you who give light to the whole world, if I am truly your son, then give me a token by which everyone may know it to be true!' At this Phoebus took off the glittering crown from his head so that Phaethon could come nearer

without being blinded. He embraced the boy and, like a true father, tried to put his mind at rest. 'Of course you are my son, and a son to be proud of, as I can see. Everything your mother told you was true, and to prove it I make you a solemn promise here and now that I will grant you whatever gift you like to ask for!'

Without a moment's hesitation Phaethon replied. He had only one wish—to drive the chariot of the sun for just one day. Immediately his father bitterly regretted the oath he had so rashly made and beat his head in agonized distress. 'My son', he pleaded, 'ask me anything but that, I beg you. This is no gift for a young boy like you. You don't know what you are asking for. No one can ride in my fiery chariot or control my horses: no man nor god can do it, not even Jupiter, and who is greater than he? Shall I tell you something about the journey? The first stage is a steep climb upwards that even the horses can scarcely manage, fresh though they are in the early morning. And when at last, after the long haul, they reach the topmost height of the sky, even I can scarcely bear to look down the sheer, empty drop to the whole world dizzily outspread below. Then comes the steep slope downwards to the west, when a strong hand is needed to rein in the horses as they plunge headlong towards the evening waters. Even Tethys, Ocean's wife, is always afraid I will come to grief in the fall. And then throughout the journey you have always to be fighting against the pull of heaven's sphere as it spins and whirls the stars in the opposite direction. I can just overcome this force but supposing that you take my chariot, will you be powerful enough to hold your own? And what about my fire-breathing horses? If it takes all my strength to control them when their blood is up and they rebel against the reins, how will *you* be able to manage them? No, my son, change your mind before it is too late. If you want proof that I am your father, you have it here: who but a father would be so anxious for your safety? How I wish you could see into my heart which aches with a father's pain! Look at all the bright world holds, all that sea and sky and land have to offer, and choose again. I would give you anything, but not this—this is no gift, but a curse!'

These warnings, terrible as they were, had no effect on Phaethon. His mind was made up and, besides, he knew his father could not go back on a solemn promise, even if he had wanted to. With a heavy heart Phoebus led the way to the coach-house where the chariot stood ready. The boy could not take his eyes off the wonderful car, with its sparkling golden wheels and silver spokes. To think it was his for a day!

By now the time of dawn was fast approaching and so the goddesses of the Hours led the fire-breathing horses of the Sun from their stables to harness them with jangling reins. Meanwhile Phoebus smeared his son's face with a sacred ointment to protect it from heat, and then placed on his head the radiant crown of the sun. In deep distress he gave his last words of advice: 'Phaethon', he said, 'if in nothing else, at least obey me in this. Use the reins, my son, not the whip. The horses need no encouragement for speed—the difficulty is to hold them back. You will see the wheel-tracks my chariot has already made through the sky. Keep to them, and do not venture too high or too low, otherwise you will scorch the sky or the earth. Steer a middle course. That is all. As for the rest, you are in the hands of Fate, and I only pray that she has more care for you than you have for yourself. But, look! Already Dawn is putting the shadows to flight.

30

It is time! Here, grasp the reins—unless, even now, I can make you change your mind and take my advice, not my chariot? Choose safety while you can, while you still stand on solid ground, and leave the world's light to me!'

But young Phaethon had already mounted the chariot. He thrilled as he took up the reins and thanked his unwilling father. Now Pyroïs and Eöus, Aëthon and Phlegon, the four horses of the sun, filled the air with their fiery whinnying and pawed the bars impatiently with their hooves. Then suddenly the bars were down and they shot forward into the vast freedom of the sky, parting the clouds as they beat their powerful wings. But they could feel no weight in the chariot behind them, no mastery in the pull of the reins, and soon, because Phaethon was so light, the chariot began to pitch and toss in the air like a ship without ballast. With no firm hand to check them, the horses ran wild and charged off the beaten track. Phaethon panicked, not knowing how to handle the reins or which way to turn. As he looked down at the world spinning round far below, his knees gave way, darkness covered his eyes and the cold chill of fear gripped his heart. Why had he ever wanted to do this? If only he had wished for something else, if only he had just stayed at home! But now what was he to do? Behind him lay a vast emptiness of sky, while far ahead lay the western horizon he would never reach. He could not drop the reins, nor yet could he hold them properly. He could not call the horses, because he did not even know their names. All around him he saw the fearful beasts of the Zodiac looming up out of the sky: Bull and Archer and Lion and Crab. Suddenly he saw the Scorpion threatening to grab him with his pincers. He dropped the reins in cold terror, and at that moment the horses bolted, pulling the chariot into the trackless deserts of the sky, and knocking against the stars in a crazy zigzag course. The Moon stood amazed as she saw her brother's horses suddenly move beneath her, scorching the clouds as they passed. The earth burst into flame as the heat came closer, and great cracks appeared in its surface so that the light penetrated down even into the underworld, striking terror into King Pluto and his court. Whole cities were burned to ashes, and along the mountain tops the forests flamed like tinder. Phaethon could no longer stand the billowing heat; the very air he breathed was like the white-hot blast of a furnace. Wrapped in a pitch-black shroud of smoke, he was swept along blindly at the mercy of the horses. This was the time, they say, when the peoples of Africa became dark-skinned as the heat made the blood rise to the surface of their bodies. Under the fierce heat, Libya was turned into dry desert and the Nile ran to hide his head at the source.

At last Mother Earth could bear no more, and pleaded with Jupiter to save the world from utter destruction. 'What have I done to deserve this?' she cried. 'The sea, too, is drying up and the sky is so white-hot that Atlas cannot support it on his shoulders much longer!' Jupiter, father of gods and men, could hesitate no more. Climbing to the top of his high tower from which he spreads out the clouds, he chose one of his mighty thunderbolts and with sure aim hurled it at Phaethon as the young charioteer whirled along in mid-career. As the bolt fell, the horses were cut free, the chariot shattered into fragments and Phaethon himself fell headlong through the air, his blazing hair streaming out behind him like the trail of a shooting star or a comet. Far from his homeland he fell, into the waters of the great river Eridanus, where nymphs gathered his charred limbs and gave him honourable burial. Phoebus his father, sick with grief, hid his face from the world for a whole day. Throughout that sunless day the world was lit only by the last flames which flickered and slowly died over the earth's surface.

6. Europa and the Bull

This little story has been second only to that of Daphne in its popularity with artists from Roman times onwards. The picture of Europa and the bull is the centrepiece of the mosaic floor to be seen at the Roman villa in Lullingstone, Kent. The owner of the villa, a prosperous man, evidently wanted to show his visitors that he was a man of learning.

The story is one of the many unflattering anecdotes about the gods which Arachne (see page 71) wove on her tapestry, thereby angering the goddess Minerva.

Minos, Europa's son, was probably a real historic character. His wife, according to legend, was Pasiphae who produced the monstrous Minotaur, half man and half bull. To house this creature Minos commissioned the craftsman Daedalus (see page 85) to build the vast maze-like building known as the labyrinth. Eventually the Minotaur was killed by the Athenian prince Theseus with the help of Ariadne, Minos' daughter. The excavations of archaeologists at the palace of Knossos in Crete have revealed that there is a basis of truth to this strange story.

'Jupiter became a bull and bellowed'—Shakespeare, *A Winter's Tale*, iv. 3.

Europa was a princess of Tyre who had the misfortune to be loved by Jupiter. The great god could not go courting in all his majesty—that would have been too frightening—so he decided to take on one of his many disguises. As usual, he called his son Mercury to his side and told him what preparations were to be made. 'My faithful Mercury', he said, 'there's not a moment to lose: you must be off down to earth this very minute on your swift wings. Make for the land of Sidon. There you will see a herd of cattle, belonging to the king, grazing on the mountain side: drive it towards the sea-shore.'

Mercury did as he was told, and soon the bullocks were being driven from their mountain pasture to the sea-shore, where Europa came every day to play with her girl companions. There Jupiter, the king of gods, lord of the thunderbolts, the mighty power who can shake the world to its foundations with a nod of his head, so far forgot his dignity as to turn himself into a bull and mingle with the herd, bellowing like the rest of them and ambling through the lush grass. What a beautiful prize bull he looked—white as the driven snow! The muscles stood out on his neck, dewlaps hung from his flanks and his little horns were a work of art, as pure and transparent as precious stone. There was no terrifying or threatening gleam in his eye—his whole expression was one of complete peace. Europa was very taken with the lovely placid animal, but at first she was frightened to approach him, tame as he was. Gradually she plucked up courage and timidly held out a handful of flowers for his lily-white muzzle to touch.

The bull was overjoyed, and licked the girl's hand to show his gratitude. He gambolled and played for her in the green meadow and
then lay on his side on the golden sands so that she could stroke his
breast and hang fresh garlands round his neck. Gradually the girl
lost all her nervousness and even ventured to sit on his back, little
knowing whose back it really was. Then the god gradually edged
away from the shore, first wading through the shallows and then
taking to the waves, heading out to sea with his prize. Poor Europa
looked back in fear and longing at the vanishing coast line, with one
hand clutching the bull's horn and the other resting on his back. Only
when they reached the island of Crete did Jupiter tell her who he was.
There, later, a son was born to Europa and Jupiter, and his name
was Minos.

7. Cadmus and the Dragon

Cadmus' city of Thebes, which began in violence, carried a curse which was to bring it more violence. Cadmus' son-in-law Pentheus aroused the anger of Dionysus by refusing to recognize him as a god, and Cadmus himself shared in the punishment by being turned into a snake. Later on, the curse passed on to King Oedipus who, without knowing it, married his mother and killed his father and then blinded himself when he discovered the truth. The story of Oedipus and his children was used by the great Greek dramatist Sophocles (5th century B.C.) for his most famous tragedies.

When Europa disappeared, her father Agenor could find no news of her whereabouts, and so he sent his son Cadmus to search for the girl, warning him that if he failed he would be punished with exile from his country. Cadmus wandered over the whole world but still he could find no trace of his sister; Jupiter was far too clever in covering up his traces. In the end, wearying of his travels, he went to the oracle to ask advice on where to settle. The oracle told him he would be guided on his way to his future home by a young heifer: when the heifer stopped and lay down in the long grass, there he was to build his city and call the place Boeotia (which in Greek means Cowfold). Cadmus had hardly left the oracle when, sure enough, he saw a young heifer in the fields. He followed it as it moved slowly across country until at last it stopped, looked back at Cadmus and his companions, raised its head, mooed gently and then sank down upon the lush grass. At once Cadmus gave thanks to the gods and bent down to kiss the ground and salute his native soil, the site where he was to build his city.

The first task was to offer sacrifice to Jupiter, and so Cadmus told his attendants to go in search of fresh spring water. They wandered into the thick forest until at length they came upon a cave, overgrown with branches and reeds. There at the mouth of the cave was a spring, bubbling up from a deep well. But in the cave behind was a ferocious dragon, terrible to look upon, with a brilliant gold crest on top of its head, flashing eyes, a huge body swollen with poisonous pus, three flickering tongues and three rows of teeth. Unfortunately, this was the very place Cadmus' attendants chose to draw water. When they dipped their pitchers into the well, clinking them against the stones, the dragon suddenly shot its head out of the mouth of the cave and let out a fearful hiss. The men dropped their pitchers and stood trembling and aghast, too frightened to move, while the dragon coiled its scaly length in writhing loops and with a sudden spring arched the upper half of its body into the air. Then it pounced, seizing some of the men with its fangs, crushing others in its enveloping folds or scorching them with the blast of its poisonous breath.

As the day drew on and his companions did not return, Cadmus set out to look for them. When at last he reached the middle of the wood and saw their bodies littered on the ground, with the dragon standing over them licking the blood from the fresh wounds, he resolved then and there to avenge their deaths or to die himself. Picking up a giant boulder he hurled it at the monster with a mighty effort. The impact would have shattered the walls of a city, but so tough was the dragon's hide that now it had no effect. Still, Cadmus' spear struck home, penetrating below the spine and sinking deep into the belly, so that the dragon twisted its head round in agony to grip

the spear with its teeth; tugging this way and that, it succeeded at last in wrenching the shaft free, but the iron tip stayed fixed deep in the bone. The monster went wild with pain, its veins swelling and its jaws slavering with poisonous foam as it painfully scraped its scaly length along the ground, fouling the air with tainted breath. It thrashed around, now coiling itself in circles, now shooting up straight as a tree, now sweeping through the forest like a river in spate. Cadmus parried its attacks with his shield, pressing his spear home in the monster's throat until at last it slowly gave ground. Cadmus drove it back upon a massive oak tree which bent with the strain as the great beast thrashed its tail. The last thrust was driven deep, and Cadmus stood above his defeated enemy in victory.

It was then that Pallas Athena, his protectress, came to Cadmus' side and told him to take the dragon's teeth and sow them in the ground: from this seed would come the harvest of a new people. Cadmus did what he was told. As he scattered the teeth in the newly ploughed furrows, an amazing thing happened. The clods of earth began to heave, and first a line of spears rose above the soil, then helmets with nodding crests, then shoulders and breastplates and armour—until a whole crop of armed warriors stood revealed above ground. It was rather like the scene in a theatre when the curtain is raised at the end of a play and you see the embroidered figures on it slowly appearing bit by bit—first their faces, then the rest of their bodies, till at last their feet rest on the stage floor.

Cadmus was terrified at the sight of this new army and prepared to defend himself, but one of the earth-born people shouted out to him. 'Put down your sword', he cried. 'This is our war, not yours!' At that, the soldier struck one of his brothers with his sword, and then fell dead himself, pierced through with a javelin. The whole crop of warriors fell upon each other in a frenzy of civil war, brother killing brother, until of all the young men granted so short a span of life only five remained: the rest lay sprawling on the bosom of their mother, Earth. One of the survivors, Echion, threw his weapons on the ground at Pallas' command, promising to fight no more if his four brothers would agree on a treaty of peace. The war ended, and it was these five brothers who joined Cadmus as his companions when he founded his city of Thebes.

When Thebes was built, Cadmus seemed to have found happiness at last. He had the daughter of two gods for a wife and she bore him many sons and daughters whose children he lived to see. But no man can be called truly happy until his last day has come: no one knows how his luck will end. So it was with Cadmus.

8. Actaeon

In this story the metamorphosis is inflicted as a punishment by the cruel and spiteful goddess Diana, the huntress. For the names of Actaeon's hounds I have used the lively Elizabethan translation by William Golding (1567). Golding's work—which was known to Shakespeare—has a real feel of the English countryside about it. His peasants, for instance, speak in a Somerset accent and here the hounds have names which a sixteenth-century English huntsman would give his pack. Notice how vividly Ovid describes Actaeon's desperate panic as he realizes he is trapped in a strange body, unable to express his feelings.

Cadmus was to know great sorrow when his grandson Actaeon met the fate I am now going to describe. Actaeon committed no crime, as you will see, unless it is a crime to lose your way. It was Fate which brought him to disaster.

One day Actaeon went out hunting with his companions. By the time midday came, the floor of the mountain forest was stained with the blood of every sort of wild beast and Actaeon was highly pleased with the morning's work. He called out to his fellow-riders: 'Our nets and spears are covered with the blood of our prey, my friends. We have had enough luck for one day. Let us call a halt and begin again by the light of tomorrow's dawn. See how the ground is already cracking under the midday heat! Take up your nets and rest!'

Some little distance from the spot where the huntsmen stopped to rest was a beautiful valley thick with pines and tapering cypress trees. This was Gargaphie, the valley sacred to Diana the huntress. Far within it lay a lovely natural grotto hollowed out of the rock: a clear spring bubbled up on the right of the arching cave and spilled out water into a grass-fringed pool. This was the haunt of Diana, who now, tired out with hunting, came to bathe her limbs in its coolness. As she stepped in she handed her spear and quiver filled with arrows to one of her attendant nymphs, while another took off her cloak and put it on her arm; a third undid her sandals while Crocale, the most skilled of them all, gathered the goddess's flowing hair into a knot. Others filled deep pitchers with water from the spring and poured it

over their mistress. It was at this moment that Actaeon came upon
the scene. After the hunt had stopped he had been wandering aim-
lessly through the woods, drawn to that grotto by the deadly power
of Fate.

As soon as he entered the dripping cave the nymphs—all uncovered
as they were—beat their breasts at the sight of a man and with
a sudden shriek clustered round Diana to veil her from sight with
their bodies. But the goddess was taller than they, and her head could
still be seen, her cheeks blushing like clouds filled by the sun's rays
or like the rosy dawn. Though her attendants crowded in around her
she stood sideways and turned her face round at the young man,
looking as though she wished her arrows were ready to hand. What
she did have at hand was water and this she scooped up and flung
over his head. 'Go now', she cried in angry prophecy, 'and tell your
story—how you saw Diana naked—if you have a voice to tell it with!'

With that, she made his sprinkled forehead swell with a stag's horns, lengthened his neck, drew out his ears to a peak, turned hands into feet and arms into long legs, and covered his body with a dappled skin. The last touch to be added was that of panic fear. Then Actaeon turned tail and fled, amazed at his own speed as he did so. As he scampered through the forest, suddenly he saw his own face and horns reflected in the water of a pool. 'Alas!' he was on the point of saying, but no words came. The only sound that would come was a groan as he felt the tears pouring down cheeks that were not his but the cheeks of a stag. But within the strange body, his mind remained the same. What was he to do? He was ashamed to return home to his palace and yet frightened to hide in the forest.

It was while he hesitated that the hounds sighted him—his own pack, trained by his own hand. Blackfoot and Stalker were the first to scent him and give call, and then the whole kennel joined in the chase: Bilbuck, Savage and Hunter; Woodman, whom a boar had but lately gored; Greediguts, with her two puppies at her heels; Blab, Fleetwood and Patch whose coat was flecked with spots; Bowman, Royster and snow-white Beauty; black-haired Tawny, plucky Tempest, Cole and Swift and gallant little Wolf with his brother pup; Snatch, who had a white star on his black forehead, and shaggy Rugg, cross-bred from a Spartan mother and Cretan father; big Jollyboy and barking Kingswood and snarling Churl and so many more that I would never have time to tell their names. The whole pack raced forward, eager for the kill, over rocks and steep crags, along rugged tracks and through the wild undergrowth, and ahead of them Actaeon fled over the hunting ground he knew so well, fled before his own hounds. 'I am Actaeon', he wanted to shout; 'I am Actaeon your master!' But the words would not rise to his lips, and only the sound of barking filled the air.

Ruffler was the first to bury his teeth in his back, then Killdeer and then Hillbred fastened on to his shoulder. Slow off the start, they had taken the lead with a short cut over the mountains, and now they held down their master while the rest of the pack raced up to sink their teeth in his flesh. Actaeon, his whole body savaged, groaned in agony—no human groan nor yet such a groan as a stag would utter. The mountain ridges echoed with his piteous cries as he fell to his knees as though in prayer, turning his eyes around and about as though stretching out his arms for mercy. But his companions, in their ignorance, urged the pack on with their huntsmen's cries while they looked about them for Actaeon. Why was he not there to enjoy the sight of the kill? 'Actaeon!' they cried, each louder than the other, and at the sound he raised his head. He was there, though well might he wish otherwise; well might he wish to see, not feel, the savagery of his hounds as they stood around him on every side, tearing their master apart. Such was the terrible vengeance of Diana: only when the poor boy's torn body breathed its last was she finally satisfied.

9. Narcissus and Echo

This is perhaps the best known of all Ovid's tales. Notice how well the story of Echo balances the story of Narcissus. While Narcissus is completely absorbed in himself and is incapable of loving others, Echo has no real personality of her own: she can only copy what other people do and say. Of the two, Ovid clearly prefers Echo, because she at least is capable of unselfish love. Medieval writers, who liked to find moral lessons in what they read, were particularly fond of this 'cautionary tale'. A popular French romance of the thirteenth century, the Roman de la Rose, translated into English by Geoffrey Chaucer speaks of

> 'The mirour perilous
> In which the proude Narcisus
> Saw al his face fair and bright.'

Soon after Narcissus was born, his mother, who was a nymph, asked the blind prophet Teiresias if her son would live long. 'He will', replied the wise old man, 'provided he does not know himself.' Narcissus' mother did not understand this mysterious prophecy at the time, but you will see from my story how it came true.

Narcissus grew up to be admired for his good looks, but he was too proud to have anything to do with other people: he preferred his own company. In fact there was only one person Narcissus really liked, and that was himself. He spent most of his time hunting deer in the forest, and it was there, one hot summer afternoon, that the nymph Echo caught sight of him. Now at that time Echo was not just a pretty voice: she had a body too, though of course her voice was just as it is today. The poor girl could never start a conversation herself, but as soon as other people started talking she could not stop repeating the last words they said. It was all because of her kind heart, really. You see, whenever the goddess Juno was close on the trail of some nymph who had been dallying with her Jupiter, Echo would buttonhole her on some excuse or other and start a long conversation, thus giving the nymph time to get away. But when Juno finally discovered she had been hoodwinked, she was furious. 'Quite a little talker, aren't you?' she sneered. 'Well, I'll soon cut your cackle.' From that day to this, poor Echo has never been able to carry on a real conversation: all she can do is repeat, pathetically, the last words she hears.

When she saw Narcissus wandering through the forest on this hot summer afternoon she fell head over heels in love, and followed softly behind him as he went. How she longed to speak to him and tell him what she felt! But this was impossible: all she could do was wait patiently until he spoke words she could repeat. By this time the boy had lost his hunting companions. 'Is there anyone here?' he called. 'Here!' cried Echo, delightedly. Narcissus stood still in amazement, looking round him to see where the voice came from, and then called louder: 'Come!' 'Come!' was Echo's eager reply. The boy looked over his shoulder but still could not see anyone. 'Why are you running away from me?' he cried. 'Why are you running away from *me*?' said Echo. Narcissus was puzzled, but he was not going to give up so easily. 'Let's meet!' he called. You can imagine how gladly Echo repeated those words. Acting on them at once, she ran out of her hiding place towards the boy, longing to put her arms round his neck. Narcissus was horrified. 'Take your hands off me!' he cried, as he took to his heels. 'I'll die sooner than let you kiss me!' 'Kiss me!' came poor

Echo's reply as she saw the boy disappearing into the depths of the forest.

After she was so cruelly jilted, Echo never showed her face again, but took to living alone in a forest cave, pining away in hopeless love. As she grieved night and day for her lost Narcissus, so her body slowly began to waste away to a skeleton until in the end nothing was left of her but her voice and her bones. People say that the bones were turned to stone, but the voice remains and is still to be heard in the woods and mountains—though Echo is seen by nobody. The only life she has is in the sound she makes.

Narcissus was to be punished for his selfishness. He had refused to return Echo's love. Very well, then, he would soon know what it feels like to love without being loved in return. One hot summer afternoon as he wandered through the forest, tired out by a morning's hunting, he came to a crystal-clear pool, lonely and silent, untouched by flocks or herds. There was fresh grass around its edge, and overhanging trees to shield it from the sun. Narcissus knelt down by the water's rim and leaned forward to quench his thirst in its delicious coolness. But as he did so he was amazed to see a beautiful face looking up at him from the surface of the pool. He was enchanted with what he saw, and lay there quite still on the bank, spellbound with delight, gazing at his own beautiful features. The foolish boy did not know that he had fallen in love with himself. Again and again he stretched out his arms to what he saw, not knowing that it was only a reflection, with no real life of its own. Narcissus was overcome with grief when he found that the loved one was beyond his reach. To think that only a thin stretch of water divided them! Nothing could tear him away from the water's edge: he lay there fascinated, slowly pining away for love of himself. He could not understand why the loved one would not come out of the pool. In the end it dawned upon him that he himself was that loved one. There was no other person there.

As the poor boy began to weep with bitter disappointment, his tears ruffled the surface of the still water so that his reflection disappeared from view in the ripples. 'Stay, don't leave me!' Narcissus cried out as he saw it go, and in his grief he tore at his tunic and beat his breast so that red bruises began to appear on his white skin. When he saw his reflected self doing the same—for by now the waters were

still again—he could not bear the cruel sight, and gradually he began
to waste away with grief as wax is melted by the sun's heat. All that
Echo had loved—his strength and glowing beauty and colour—slowly
faded away. Echo saw what had happened and though she was still
angry at the memory of how she had been treated, her heart was
moved with pity. As the dying boy groaned, she groaned in reply,
and as he beat his arms in grief, she beat hers. His last words as he
gazed into the water were 'Alas for the one I loved in vain', and poor
Echo could only reply, with some truth, 'I have loved in vain.'

So Narcissus died, and passed into the underworld. They say that
down there he is still gazing at his reflection in the waters of the river
Styx. His sisters, the nymphs of the spring, prepared a funeral for him
and sang laments, with Echo answering in refrain, but when they
came to bury his body, it was nowhere to be found. In its place was
a flower of white and yellow petals. Men call it the narcissus to
this day.

10. Pyramus and Thisbe

This is not a Greek myth but a story which came to Ovid from an eastern source, perhaps from Babylon. The mention of the burst water-pipe is more comic than tragic. Shakespeare poked fun at this story in *A Midsummer Night's Dream*, where it is the subject of the play performed by Bottom the weaver and his band of rustic players.

Long ago in the sun-baked city of Babylon there was a boy and a girl called Pyramus and Thisbe. These two lived next door to each other and as they grew older they came to love one another dearly. They wanted to get married but their parents would have none of it and kept them apart: they could only speak their love by secret signs. Now there was a crack in the wall which divided their two houses which no one had noticed before. The two lovers in their desperation were quick to discover it and through this chink they would whisper their love when all was quiet, each on either side of the wall. 'Cruel wall', they would say, 'Why do you keep us apart? Couldn't you let us have just one kiss? Not that we're ungrateful. If it wasn't for you we would not be able to talk to each other at all.' So Pyramus and Thisbe murmured their love through the wall that divided them.

Early one morning, while the dew was still wet upon the grass, they came to the chink to share their sorrows. At last they decided that very night they would give their guardians the slip, steal out of the town and meet near Ninus' tomb! So that evening, soon after nightfall, Thisbe tiptoed out of her house, turning the door ever so gently on its hinge, and veiling her face she made her way to Ninus' tomb, where she sat down beneath the shade of the mulberry tree, waiting for Pyramus. Suddenly by the light of the moon she saw a lioness coming out of the darkness to quench its thirst at the spring and to wash the blood of freshly killed prey from its jaws. In her terror Thisbe ran to take shelter in a cave, and as she ran she let fall her veil. This veil the lioness found and tore to pieces, covering it with blood.

48

Meanwhile Pyramus had been late in escaping from his home, and when at last he reached the tree the first thing he saw was Thisbe's veil, all torn and blood-stained, while Thisbe was nowhere to be seen. He clasped the veil to himself. In an agony of despair and grief: 'O Thisbe', he moaned, 'why did I bring you out here to your death? Why was I not here in time to meet you? At least you shall not die alone!' At that he drew his sword and plunged it into his breast. As he fell back the blood spurted up on to the tree, like a jet spouting from a burst pipe. That was when the mulberry fruit first got its purple stain.

Hardly had the deed been done when Thisbe ventured timidly out of the cave, fearful of the lioness but longing to find Pyramus and tell him of her lucky escape. As she looked around in the dark, at first she could not recognize the tree and its stained fruit, but then she saw the body and turned pale, trembling like the sea when its surface is rippled by the breeze. Tearing her hair and beating her breast she mingled her tears in Pyramus' blood, embracing his lifeless corpse. 'I am the cause of this!' she cried, as she recognised her veil and saw Pyramus' empty scabbard. 'But like your love, mine will be true to death. Our parents would not let us be united in life, at least they will not forbid us to share a grave. The mulberry shall always bear the marks of our death, its fruit coloured for ever by the blood we shed'. So saying, she fell upon the sword, still warm from the blood of the lover she had met at last, in death.

11. Perseus

The hero who rescues damsels in distress is to be found in the folklore of every country and every age. St. George and Sir Lancelot are two examples that spring immediately to mind—not forgetting, in more recent times, the resourceful Batman. One cannot help feeling that Ovid sometimes has a quiet laugh at Perseus' expense. Our hero always does the correct thing, even remembering to ask Andromeda's parents for formal permission to take their daughter's hand in marriage when they are all in imminent danger from the dragon.

The dramatic scene of Perseus' rescue was often painted by artists. The painting by Piero di Cosimo, shown above hangs in the Uffizi gallery, Florence. Notice that more than one episode is illustrated, and Perseus and Andromeda appear several times.

You all know the story of the hero Perseus and how he was sent on a mission to kill the terrible Medusa, whose gaze turned all living things to stone. This Medusa lived in a rocky stronghold guarded by two old hags who shared the use of one eye. But Perseus outwitted them by stealing away the eye just as it was being passed by hand from one to the other, and so slipped through unseen. As he advanced he could see everywhere around him the frozen shapes of men and beasts turned to flint by Medusa's dreadful stare, but he approached the monster, avoiding her eyes by looking at her reflection mirrored in the round burnished shield he held in his left hand. When she fell into a sound sleep he grasped her head, all intertwined as it was with snakes, cut it off and carried it away through the air. As he flew, some drops of blood from Medusa's head fell upon the ground, and from this seed there arose a wonderful winged horse named Pegasus. Other drops gave birth to all sorts of snakes, and this is how the earth came to be filled with that crawling breed of reptiles.

Perseus flew on and on until evening began to fall and, fearing to trust the darkness, he called a halt for the night in the western kingdom of Atlas, hoping to rest there until dawn. This Atlas was the most enormous giant who has ever lived, lord of vast dominions on the edge of the western world, and master of the seas into which the sun's weary horses plunge at evening. Thousands upon thousands of flocks and herds fed upon his wide pastures, and there were no neighbours to threaten his borders. In his possession was a wonderful golden tree from whose glittering leafy branches hung golden fruit. Perseus

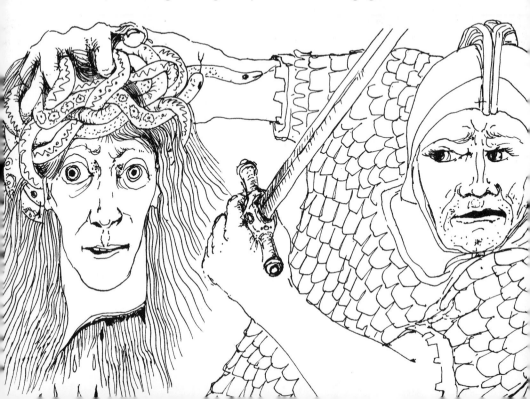

approached the giant. 'My friend', he said, 'may I introduce myself?
It may interest you to know that I am the son of Jupiter. I have done
famous deeds, too, if you admire that sort of thing. Will you be kind
enough to give me welcome and shelter?' But Atlas remembered an
ancient prophecy, which said that one day his golden tree would be
robbed by a son of Jupiter. It was for that reason that he had surrounded his orchard with high mountains and had set a huge dragon
on guard there, to frighten off all strangers. He was not pleased to
see Perseus. 'Be off with you!' he cried, 'or you won't have much to
boast about by the time I've finished with you!' With that he began
to use violence and thrust Perseus away, though our hero protested
and tried to reason with the giant, grappling all the while. But it was
no good—who could be a match for Atlas in strength? 'Very well,
then,' said Perseus. 'If you don't want my gratitude, here is a present
for you.' And with that, he turned his own face away and with his

53

left hand held out the snaky head of Medusa. There and then Atlas turned into a mountain of equally gigantic size. His beard and hair were transformed into forests, his shoulders and hands into ridges, his bones into rocks, and what had been his head was now a mountaintop. Then he expanded in all directions (it was the gods who decided this), so that his vast bulk supported the whole sky with its millions of stars.

Soon the morning star rose bright in the sky, warning men to be about their day's work, and Aeolus, lord of the tempests, called his winds back into their prison. Perseus strapped his wings to both feet, and buckling on his curved sword sailed once more into the air on his winged sandals. He passed over countries without number until at last he saw far below him the lands of Ethiopia and kingdom of Cepheus. Here a beautiful girl called Andromeda had been chained fast to a rock by the unjust command of Jupiter Ammon—all because her mother had been too boastful of her beauty. The girl looked for all the world like a marble statue—except that her delicate hair

54

stirred in the light breeze and warm tears ran down her face. Perseus was suddenly so struck with her beauty that he almost missed a beat of his wings. He did not know it, but he was in love. 'Maiden', he said, 'you deserve no bonds, except those of marriage. Tell me your name and country. What is the reason for these chains?' Andromeda was too shy to reply at first and would have covered her face with her hands, if they had not been tied behind her back. All she could do was weep. But when Perseus persisted, she was afraid he would take her silence for an admission of guilt, so she told him her name and country and how her mother had rashly boasted of her beauty. She was still telling her story when suddenly the sea began to thunder and out of it appeared a huge monster, breasting the waves for miles around. Andromeda shrieked with fear, and her poor mother and father wept and moaned as they clung to her, chained on the rock. Perseus thought quickly. 'There is no time for tears now', he said to them. 'If we are to act there is not a minute to lose. I will be brief. I am Perseus and I want to marry your daughter. I have much to recommend me. Jupiter is my father and you may have heard how I

overcame the snaky Gorgon and dared to fly through the air on my winged feet. In the ordinary way you would welcome such a son-in-law with open arms, but with the gods' help I will do still more for you. If I save your daughter from the dragon, will you let her be mine?' Andromeda's parents did not hesitate an instant: they begged Perseus to help them, promising in addition to give him their whole kingdom as a dowry.

By this time the monster was advancing breast-high, churning up a wake on either side like a ship rowed at full speed by a strong and sweaty crew. It was already a stone's throw from the rock when Perseus soared up into the clouds. Seeing his shadow on the water's surface, the monster struck out at it and then Perseus plummeted down from the sky to drive his sword deep into his enemy's back, just as an eagle pounces on a snake sunning itself in an empty field, and fastens its greedy claws into the creature's scaly neck. Mad with agony, the monster now towered up into the air, now dived beneath the water, now thrashed around like a wild boar beset by a pack of howling dogs. With his swift wings Perseus escaped the attacks of its ugly, snapping jaws and wielded his sword wherever there was an opening: he lunged now at its back, all caked with sea-shells, then at its ribs, then at its fishy tail. The beast spewed up quantities of sea-water mingled with dark-red blood so that Perseus' feathers were drenched with spray. No longer daring to trust his dripping wings, the hero made for a rock which jutted out of the water not far away. Leaning against it, and holding on to the cliff edge with his left hand, he plunged his sword three and four times into the beast's entrails until it fell defeated at last. Deafening applause broke out along the shore and even in the houses of the gods above. Andromeda's parents were overjoyed and went to greet their new son-in-law, calling him the rescuer and saviour of their home. The girl herself, the cause and the reward of his ordeal, was freed from her chains.

Perseus washed his victorious hands in the sea water and then gently laid the Medusa's head on a soft bed of leaves and seaweed, so that it should not come to harm on the hard beach. This seaweed, still fresh and absorbent, soaked up the power of the monster so that it became hard and stiff. The sea-nymphs were amazed at the miracle and to try it out they did the same with more and more seaweed,

touching the Medusa's head with it and then scattering the seeds over the waves.

This was the origin of coral, which has remained the same to this very day: beneath the water it is a plant, while above the water it turns into stone upon contact with the air.

There on the site of his victory, Perseus built three altars of fresh turf, one to Mercury, one to Minerva and between them one to Jupiter. To Mercury he sacrificed a bullock, to Minerva a cow and to Jupiter, greatest of the gods, a bull. Then he claimed Andromeda as his reward and bride. The marriage torches were lit, the scent of incense filled the air, and the whole palace echoed to the merry sound of flute and lyre as the marriage song was raised. The golden doors of Cepheus' palace swung open to admit everyone to the feast, and Perseus took Andromeda for his bride.

12. Ceres and Proserpine

This is one of the most ancient of the Greek myths, with its account of how the year came to be divided into winter and summer. (We must remember that the contrast between winter and summer is quite violent in some parts of Greece.) Ceres (the Greeks called her Demeter) was the goddess who represented Mother Earth, the source of all fruitfulness. In the British Museum there is a beautiful statue which dates from the fourth century B.C. showing Demeter seated, mourning for her daughter. The picture below

is from a medieval French manuscript. The story, with its rich wealth of meaning, has inspired many poets, including our own John Milton who wrote of

> 'that fair field
> Of Enna, where Proserpine gathering flowers,
> Herself a fairer flower, by gloomy Dis
> Was gathered, which cost Ceres all that pain
> To seek her through the world.'

Ceres is the goddess of fruitfulness and rich harvests. It was she who first disturbed the earth's soil with the plough and taught men how to plant corn and reap it for their bread. This is her story, and the story of her daughter Proserpine, who was lost.

It all began when the giant Typhoeus challenged the gods and tried to scale the heights of heaven. As a punishment, his body was buried beneath the massive weight of the enormous island of Sicily, though he struggled all the while. His huge head was buried beneath Mount Etna and belched up sand and flame through its top. Lying on his back, smothered by the mass above him, he struggled to roll away the towns and great mountains that crushed his body. The quaking of the earth terrified the lord of the silent underworld, Pluto, who was afraid that the earth's surface would crack wide open and let the daylight into his kingdom of the shades. Such a disaster had to be avoided at all costs, so Pluto left his dark haunts beneath the earth and in a chariot pulled by four black horses drove round the island of Sicily to inspect its foundations. He made certain that there were no weak points, but as he made his rounds he was seen by the goddess Venus, from her shrine on the mountain of Eryx. At once she went to seek the help of her son, the winged young god of love. 'Cupid', she said, putting her arms round him, 'what would I do without you? All my power is worked through you. With your irresistible arrows of love you have conquered Jupiter and the gods above, you have conquered the spirits of the sea, too, and Neptune their master. Only the third and last kingdom of the world has still to be overcome by the power of love—the underworld, whose master, Pluto, you can see down there, riding round Sicily in his hellish chariot. Take one of your conquering arrows, my son, and shoot it straight at Pluto's breast! We must do something to restore our reputation. Even in heaven, the power of love is not what it used to be. Pallas Athene and Diana have already escaped us, and it will be the same with Ceres' daughter Proserpine unless we hurry. You must arrange a marriage between Proserpine and her uncle Pluto!'

When his mother had finished, Cupid opened his quiver and from his thousand arrows chose the sharpest, the surest and the most obedient. Then he bent the curving bow back against his knee and let fly the shaft, piercing Pluto to the heart.

Now in the island of Sicily, not far from Henna's walls, there is a deep lake which echoes to the call of swans and is fringed on every side by trees which veil the waters from the sun's rays. Every kind of flower grows wild on the cool, shady banks, where Spring never ends. Here Proserpine was playfully gathering violets and lilies with her friends, each girl competing with the others to see who could pick the

most. It was here that Pluto saw her and, on seeing her, swept her off on the spot—so strong was his love. In terror, Proserpine called out for her mother and friends—for her mother especially. As she tore her dress, the flowers she had gathered tumbled from its folds so that for all her fear, the sight of such waste still made her cry. But Pluto's chariot gathered speed as he urged on each of his horses by name and shook the black reins. On and on they went, across deep lakes and pools that bubbled with sulphur, until they reached a narrow inlet where the sea is enclosed by jutting headlands. The nymph to whom these waters belonged, Cyane, now rose waist-high from the waves and blocked Pluto's path. 'You won't get past me!' she cried. 'You cannot marry Proserpine against her mother's will—I call this kidnapping, not courting! Look at me, now. Someone was in love with me, long ago. His name was Anapus. I married him because he asked me nicely, not because he frightened me into it!' With these words she stretched wide her arms to bar the way. Pluto, containing his anger no longer, promptly turned his savage horses downwards into the depths of the pool, hurling his royal sceptre to the bottom with such force that it broke open a way to the underworld through which his chariot dived headlong. Then Cyane, overcome with grief, dissolved into tears. Her limbs began to give way, her bones grew soft, her nails lost their hardness. The slenderest parts of her body—hair, fingers, legs—were the first to become liquid, and then it was the turn of shoulders, back, sides and breast: all vanished into the flowing water. From being the nymph of the pool, Cyane turned into the pool itself.

Meanwhile Ceres was searching every land and sea, panic-stricken at the loss of her daughter. Dawn found her still searching and so did Evening. When darkness fell she lit two pine-torches from the fires of Etna and carried them tirelessly through the frosty shadows of the night. Again when the gentle day dulled the light of the stars she continued the search for Proserpine from east to west. Her lips were already parched with thirst when she came upon a poor, thatched cottage and knocked at its low door. An old woman came out and seeing the goddess gave her a drink of sweet water, sprinkled with roasted barley. While Ceres drank it gratefully, a bold, cheeky boy came up and laughed. 'Greediguts!' he cried, cocking a snook at the

goddess. Enraged by the insult she promptly flung what was left of the water and barley meal into his face, cutting short his words. As it soaked in, his face began to come out in spots, his arms suddenly turned into legs, a tail sprouted for good measure and his whole body shrank to a harmless size, smaller even than a lizard. The poor old woman was amazed and burst into tears but as she tried to touch it, the creature scuttled off down a hole. Because it is starred with spots, men call it a stellion now.

This, then, was how the stellion got its spots. Meanwhile Ceres was continuing her search across more lands and seas than I could ever have time to tell. On her journey she came to the pool of Cyane and if only the nymph had not been changed she would have told the whole story: she longed to speak out, but try as she might, she could find no tongue with which to speak. However at the moment when Pluto's chariot had dived down into the pool, Proserpine had dropped her girdle, and Cyane now let this girdle float to the surface of her waters, as a clear sign to the goddess. When Ceres saw it, she began to tear her hair and beat her breast as if realizing for the first time what had happened to her daughter. But where was Proserpine? Her mother still did not know. In her anger she began to abuse the earth, calling it ungrateful and unworthy of her gift of corn, but no land did she abuse more bitterly than Sicily, the island which bore the traces of her daughter's loss. There with her own hand she broke up the ploughs, put farmers and cattle to death, rotted the seed, and ruined the harvest. The island's rich, world-famous cornfields lay barren, and its crops failed with the violence of sun and rain and wind.

It was at this point that Arethusa came to the rescue. Now Arethusa was nymph of a spring which rose in Sicily but had its source in Greece, travelling many hundreds of miles under sea and land before rising to the surface in a bubbling fountain. Lifting her head from her waters and smoothing back her dripping hair behind her ears, she began to plead with Ceres. 'Mother of crops', she said, 'who have searched for your daughter throughout the whole world, it is time for you to rest from your vast efforts. Do not be in a rage against your faithful Sicily. It has done nothing wrong! How could it resist Pluto? I am not pleading for my own country, because I am only a guest in Sicily: my real home and source is in Elis. Yet I love Sicily more than any other land—be kind to it and protect it. Later on, when your worries are at an end and you are in the mood for listening, I will tell you how I came to travel all those many miles underground to my spring, here in Ortygia. For the moment, let me only tell you this: that as I glided through the underworld by the streams of Styx, I saw your Proserpine with my own eyes. Sad, yes, and frightened she may be, but still a queen, mistress of the shades and wife to the lord of hell!'

Ceres stood stock still in amazement at these words. Then, when her grief had given way to bitter indignation, she was up and away in her chariot to the heights of heaven. There she stood before the throne of Jupiter, her hair all dishevelled, and vented her indignation and hate. 'Proserpine is your daughter as well as mine,' she said to Jupiter. 'If you have no love left for me, then at least think of her. Do not value her less, simply because I am her mother! I have searched high and low for her, and at last I have found her—if "finding" means knowing where she is. I could forgive Pluto for stealing her—if only he would return her to me safe and sound! Is your daughter to be married to a robber?' 'My dear', replied Jupiter, 'I love and care for Proserpine as much as you do, but you don't understand. Pluto has committed no crime—this is love. If you give your consent to this marriage, he won't disappoint you as a son-in-law. He has many things to recommend him—after all not many gods can claim to be Jupiter's brother, and he ranks only second after me! However, if you are so anxious to keep them apart, I will allow Proserpine to return above the earth, but on one condition: her lips must have touched no food in the underworld. That is laid down by the Fates!'

Ceres still insisted that her daughter should be returned, but it was not to be, for the girl had already eaten of the fruits of Pluto's kingdom. As she wandered through his well-kept gardens she had plucked a pomegranate from an overhanging tree, and taking seven seeds from its pale husk had placed them in her mouth. No one would have known, but she was seen by Ascalaphus the son of Orphne, a nymph of the underworld, and the heartless man told what he had seen, thereby robbing Proserpine of her chance of return. As a punishment she turned him into a bird, sprinkling his head with water from the underworld river so that it developed a beak and feathers and large round eyes: losing his human shape, he began to sprout tawny wings and long curved claws. He had become a screech-owl, that horrid bird of ill-omen whose dreadful cry foretells coming disaster.

Jupiter now had to come between his brother and his angry sister. To settle their dispute he divided the year's cycle into two. For six months from April until September Proserpine stays on earth with her mother, and for six months from October until March she stays in the underworld with her husband. While she lives below, she is sad and gloomy, but when the time comes for her to rise up into the light of day she meets her mother with such a radiant smile that the sun comes out to shine and winter's clouds are put to flight.

64

13. Arethusa

This is one of those stories invented to explain the origin of a real place—in this case the fountain of Ortygia which is on the island of Sicily, at Syracuse. Many of the Syracusan coins, which were the finest in the Greek world, bore the image of Arethusa, the nymph of this fountain.

Ovid is unsurpassed in his description of clear streams and river scenes. Perhaps he was thinking of the countryside round his own home at Sulmo, beneath the Apennine hills. In another poem he tells that his boyhood was spent where

> 'Sulmo lies amid Pelignian hills,
> Small, but for ever fresh with watering rills. . . .
> Pelignian fields with trickling streams abound,
> And luscious herbage clothes the softened ground.'
>
> (*Amores* ii. 16. 1–2, 5–6, transl. by L. P. Wilkinson)

Milton has two lovely lines which suggest that the river god eventually found a means of following Arethusa. He speaks of

> 'Divine Alpheus, who by secret sluice
> Stole under seas to meet his Arethuse.'
>
> (*Arcades*, 31–2)

When Ceres had recovered her daughter safe and sound she went back to hear Arethusa's story, curious to know the reason for her long journey beneath the earth. When she arrived at the spring, the waters fell silent as the nymph lifted her head above their surface, wringing the moisture from her blue-green hair. At last Arethusa told her story of long-ago love. 'Once', she said, 'I was one of the nymphs who live in the Greek land of Achaea. No one loved hunting more keenly than I, but although I never looked for praise, although mine was a life of action, I was famous for my beauty. Not that this gave me any pleasure, for while it would have delighted other girls to hear their

65

charms praised so much, I could only blush like the simple country lass I was, and thought it wrong to be so admired.

'One day—how clearly it all comes back to me!—I was returning from the Stymphalian wood, tired by a long day's hunting in the heat. As I walked under the burning sun I came to a lovely stream that flowed with hardly a ripple or murmur—so clear that you could count every pebble on the sandy bottom, so still that you could hardly detect the current. On the sloping banks, silvery willows and poplars provided a natural and delicious shade. I went up to the edge and ever so gently tried out the cool water, first with the tip of my toe, then up to the knee. Not content with that I took off my clothes, hung them on a willow branch and dived into the stream. I struck out and pulled in with my arms, gliding and shaking and splashing with a thousand different strokes until with sudden horror I heard a murmur rise from beneath the middle of the stream. I made for the nearer bank and stood there in terror. "Where are you off to, Arethusa?" came a hoarse voice. It was the river-god himself, Alpheus! "Arethusa," he called again, "where are you off to?" At that I bolted, though without my clothes, for they were on the other bank. But the faster I ran, the more hotly and fiercely he pursued me, like a hawk on the tail of a fluttering dove. Over hill and mountain I ran, always just keeping beyond his grasp, over plains and rocks and trackless deserts. The sun was behind me and I could see his long shadow stretching in front of my feet—or was it my frightened imagination? The sound of his running was enough to terrify me, certainly, and his powerful panting which blew upon my hair. I was exhausted by the chase. "Diana," I cried, "my protectress! Help me! I am caught! Remember how I used to follow you in the hunt and carried your bow and quiver of arrows!" My prayer touched the goddess's heart so that she took one of her thick clouds and wrapped it round me just before Alpheus had time to catch up. The river-god was quite put off his stride and went round and round the cloud in search of me. Twice without knowing it he passed the place where the goddess had hidden me. "Ho there! Arethusa!" he called. "Arethusa, ho there!" Can you imagine what I felt like? Like a lamb, perhaps, that hears the wolves howling around the high sheepfold? Or like a hare hidden in a thorn bush which can see the muzzles of its pursuers and dares not make a move? If only he would go away! But he saw that my footprints went no farther and so stayed, guarding the cloud which hid me. Trapped as I was, I could feel a cold sweat breaking out over my limbs. Then greenish drops began to trickle all over my body. Wherever I moved my feet, the ground began to run with water, moisture poured from my hair and in less time than I need to tell this story I was changed into a stream. But stream though I was, Alpheus still recognized me and, not to be outwitted, at once turned himself back into his own stream so as to mingle his waters with mine. But he had reckoned without Diana. She burst open the ground and I dropped deep down into the cavernous depths below. And that was how I came to Ortygia. It was there, on this lovely island of Sicily, that I first rose to the surface from my long passage through the world beneath.'

14. Arachne

This is a story designed to explain the origin of the spider. As in the stories of Lycaon and Actaeon the metamorphosis or change of shape is inflicted as a punishment by an angry goddess.

The episode gives Ovid the opportunity to tell several 'stories within a story' by describing the scenes woven by Minerva and Arachne on their tapestries. This was a favourite device of epic poets, following Homer's *Iliad* where there is a famous passage describing the scenes decorated on Achilles' shield by Hephaestus, the blacksmith of the gods.

No one was more skilled at spinning and weaving than the goddess Minerva. She invented the craft herself. Imagine her anger, then, when she heard that her skill had been insulted by an ordinary mortal woman called Arachne, who said that she, not Minerva, was the best spinner in the world. This Arachne came from a humble home in Libya and her father had been a dyer. As the child grew up she became famous throughout the district for her skill at the loom, poor though she was. Even the nymphs would leave the slopes of their vine-clad hills to come down and watch her at work, winding the coarse yarn into balls, or softening it with her fingers into long fleecy strands of wool, or deftly twisting her slender spindle to and fro, or embroidering the finished cloth with her needle. You could tell that she had been taught by the great Minerva herself—and yet this was what Arachne steadfastly refused to admit. She was so annoyed at the suggestion that anyone, even a goddess, could have been her teacher that she challenged Minerva to a weaving contest. 'If the goddess wins', she declared, 'she can do what she likes with me.'

So Minerva disguised herself as an old white-haired woman. Hobbling along on a stick she came up to Arachne and gave her a warning. 'Old people aren't entirely useless, you know,' she said. 'They know life from experience. So I'm going to give you a piece of advice, Arachne my girl. Boast as much as you like of your skill compared with other mortal women, but never seek to rival a goddess. Go on, beg Minerva for forgiveness: she will grant it if you ask her nicely.' Arachne glared furiously at the old woman and flew into such

a temper that she could hardly refrain from striking her. 'You sense-
less old hag', she cried. 'The only thing you're fit for is the grave. Go
off and give your advice to your daughter or your daughter-in-law,
if you have one! I don't need any advice from you, and you needn't
think that it has had the slightest effect. I don't take back a word I
said. Anyway, why doesn't Minerva come and take up my challenge?'
'But she has come', came the answer, and with that Minerva shed her
old woman's disguise and revealed herself in all her glory. The
women around bowed in amazement and reverence—all, that is,
except Arachne, who wasn't in the least frightened, though she
blushed faintly. The obstinate woman persisted in her challenge,
and eagerness for victory blinded her to the disaster she was courting.
Minerva gave up all attempt at persuasion, and prepared for the
contest without more ado.

The contestants then set up their looms, one at each end of the great hall. They stretched out the slender threads, tied the frames to the crossbeams and with nimble fingers began to weave the cross-threads through the warp by using their pointed shuttles, each thread set firmly in place by a blow from the comb. With their skirts hitched up, the goddess and the girl worked away with a will, forgetting the labour in their enthusiasm for their skilful task. Into the cloth they wove threads dyed purple in Tyrian coppers and other colours of the rainbow—so subtly different that you could scarcely see where one shaded into another. Gold braid, too, was woven into the cloth, and each tapestry told a different story.

The scene Minerva embroidered on her tapestry was the famous contest held at Athens between herself and Neptune to decide what name that city should have. There to judge the contest were twelve gods seated in majesty upon the Acropolis, with Jupiter in their midst. There was Neptune standing up and striking the rocks with his long trident: his claim to the city was the sea which came gushing out of the cleft. Minerva represented herself in full armour with shield, spear, helmet and aegis: she had just struck the ground with her spear and out of it was sprouting a grey-green olive tree, loaded with berries. The victory was hers, and the city was named Athens after the name by which the Greeks knew her: Athene. Minerva added four scenes to illustrate what reward Arachne might expect for her impudence. The scenes showed the punishment meted out to other mortals who had dared to rival the gods. One cover showed Haemon and Rhodope—once humans but now turned into icy mountains for laying claim to the greatness of godhead. There too was the queen of the pygmies whom Juno defeated and turned into a crane to wage war against her own people. Another rival of Juno—Antigone—was in the third corner, changed by the jealous goddess into a white-winged stork, still applauding herself with clattering beak. The last scene showed Cinyras, weeping as he lay on the temple steps which had once been his daughters' limbs. This completed the design, and round the edge Minerva wove a frieze of olive leaves, the symbol of peace, finishing the whole work by depicting her own tree.

Arachne's tapestry showed far different scenes. With mischievous impudence she showed the gods in love. There was Jupiter in all the many disguises he used to deceive mortal women. As a bull he was carrying Europa out to sea while the frightened girl looked back at the disappearing land, crying out to her companions and timidly shrinking from the waves breaking around her feet: you would have thought that the bull and the waves were real, so lifelike was the picture. Arachne showed Jupiter in other shapes, too: as an eagle, a swan, a shower of gold, a flame, a shepherd, a spotted snake—all disguises assumed in the cause of love. Then she embroidered the loves of Neptune, who appeared now as a bull, now as a horse, now as a dolphin and now as a bird. Nor was Phoebus forgotten in the tapestry, nor Bacchus, nor Saturn: the loves of all the famous gods were there for all to see, and round them Arachne wove a design of colourful flowers entwined with ivy.

When Minerva saw Arachne's beautiful tapestry she could not contain herself for jealousy and anger. How dare this upstart woman depict the secrets of the gods? She tore down the beautiful web and then struck Arachne three and four times with her shuttle. The poor

woman at last could not take any more punishment and in despair put a noose round her neck, intending to hang herself. As she dangled there on the rope Minerva took pity on her at last and lifted her up. 'You wicked girl,' she said, 'I cannot let you die like this. You shall live but for ever hang like this in mid-air. This, too, will be the fate of all your descendants!' At that she sprinkled Arachne with the juice of magic herbs. The poor girl's hair and ears vanished at their touch, her head shrank in size and her whole body became smaller. Her slender fingers remained stuck to her sides to be used as legs but all the rest of her was belly. From that belly she still spins her thread and weaves her web today, no more a woman but a spider.

15. Jason and Medea

The story of Jason and the Argonauts was popular with Greek writers. Several Greek and Roman dramatists wrote tragedies about Medea. Ovid uses all his powers of rhetoric (see introduction) to describe the inner conflict of Medea as she debates with herself whether or not to help Jason. The description of Medea's midnight sorcery is one of the most haunting in all the *Metamorphoses*. It was used by Shakespeare when he came to write Prospero's magic incantation in *The Tempest*: 'Ye elves of hills, brooks, standing lakes and groves. . . .'

You have all heard the story of how Jason and his companions set sail in the Argo to find and bring back the golden fleece. They had many difficulties and dangers on the way, but at last they reached their destination, the land of Colchis. Jason lost no time in approaching the King of Colchis and asked him to give back the golden fleece. The king, whose name was Aeëtes, said he would only return the fleece on three conditions. First, Jason must harness the king's bulls to the yoke; then, after ploughing the ground he must sow in it the teeth of a dragon; lastly, he had to get past the terrible serpent which mounted guard over the golden tree on which the fleece hung.

While Jason stood before the king, he was closely watched by the king's daughter Medea, a sorceress who possessed magic powers. Medea, in spite of herself, felt strangely drawn towards the young Greek. 'Can this be what they call love?' she said to herself. 'It is certainly something very like it. There is no use in resisting the gods. Why do I find my father's demands so cruel? Am I afraid for the life of a man I have hardly seen? I can see that I ought to support my father and yet I cannot! Unless I help Jason he will be blasted by the breath of the fiery bulls, or killed by the seed he sows, or eaten by the serpent which guards the golden fleece. And yet am I to betray my father for a stranger, who will only sail away and leave me here alone? But I can see that Jason is not a man like that. How noble and handsome he looks! I will save him, and he will marry me and I will sail away from this barbarous land for ever.

'With Jason by my side, I will never fear the dangers of the journey, those whirlpools and clashing rocks. The only fear I shall feel will be for my husband. Did I say "husband"? Oh, Medea, how quick you are to think of excuses for doing wrong! Remember your duty to your father and country and do not be tempted!'

These were the thoughts that conflicted within Medea's mind. In the end she had made up her mind to be faithful to her father and was on her way to offer sacrifice at Hecate's altar in the forest (Hecate was the goddess of sorcery) when she caught sight of Jason again. He happened to be looking even more handsome than usual that day, so you can understand when I tell you that she fell in love all over again: her passion revived like an ember fanned into flame by the wind. Taking her hand and speaking softly Jason begged for her help and promised he would marry her. With the tears streaming down her cheeks she replied, 'I see what I must do. It is wrong, but it is love, not ignorance that commands. I will save you, only keep your promise afterwards!' Then Jason swore a solemn oath by Hecate and by the all-seeing godhead of the Sun, after which Medea gave him her magic herbs by which he was to be saved, and told him how to use them.

The next day in the morning the whole people flocked to the field of Mars and took up their stand on the slopes. In the midst of the throng sat the king himself, dressed in a purple robe and carrying his ivory sceptre. But look! There already were the brazen-hoofed bulls breathing fire through their nostrils of steel so that the grass withered at the touch of their breath. From their parched throats came the roar of the furnace that raged within their breasts. But Jason went to meet them. They swung round savagely to face him with a toss of

their iron-tipped horns and pawed the ground fiercely with cloven hoofs, uttering bellows mixed with clouds of smoke. Jason's companions went stiff with fright, but still he went towards them, not feeling the fire because of the magic ointment Medea had given him. He stretched out his hand boldly to fondle their hanging dewlaps and then yoked them and drove the heavy team forward, ploughing the soil. The Colchians were amazed while Jason's companions encouraged him on with cheers.

Then Jason took the dragon's teeth from a bronze helmet and scattered them over the ploughed fields. These seeds which had been soaked beforehand in strong poison were softened by the soil and at once began to swell into new and strange shapes. Just as a baby takes shape in its mother's womb and emerges into the world fully formed, so the earth's teeming womb gave birth to perfect, full-grown human bodies. More amazing still, as soon as they appeared they began to brandish weapons of war. When Jason's companions saw these warriors poising their sharp spears ready to hurl them at the hero, their hearts sank and even Medea went pale with fright, and lest her herbs should not prove strong enough she chanted an extra spell to help him. Then Jason hurled a stone into the midst of his enemies, which made them turn away from him and start fighting among themselves: the earth-born brotherhood fell upon each other in bloody civil war until not one was left alive. The Greeks rushed out to congratulate their victorious leader and hugged him for joy. Medea would have done the same if she could, but shame and the thought of what people would say held her back. But what secret joy she nursed in her heart! How she thanked her magic spells and the gods from whom they came!

One task remained: to put to sleep the ever-watchful sentry of the golden tree—the frightful crested serpent with his three-forked tongue and fang-like teeth. Jason was not deterred. He sprinkled the monster with juice from a narcotic herb and then three times chanted a soothing spell, the spell by which seas are calmed and swollen rivers are stilled. For the first time the serpent's eyes closed in sleep and Jason seized his golden prize to carry it off in triumph.

So Jason sailed home to Iolcos, carrying with him the golden fleece and the woman who had helped him to win it. All the people of

Iolcos were there to welcome the hero and his new wife—all except his old father Aeson who was now feeble with age. Jason was so touched with pity that he now asked Medea to use her magic powers by taking away some of his own years of life and adding them to his father's. Medea was deeply moved to think that a son could show such devotion. She thought of her own father Aeëtes and how she had abandoned him. But she pretended to be shocked at her husband's suggestion. 'How can you think of such a thing, Jason?' she said. 'Hecate would never allow it. I will try to prolong your father's life—not by taking away your years, however, but by using my magic arts with the help of the three-fold goddess.'

Three nights later when the moon was full, Medea arose and went out of the palace in flowing robes, her feet bare, her hair streaming

over her shoulders. She was alone in the deep stillness of the night. Even the leaves were motionless, and the damp air. Only the stars sparkled with movement. Stretching her arms towards them, three times Medea turned round in a circle, three times she took water from a stream and poured it on her hair, three times she howled aloud. 'O Night,' she prayed, kneeling on the hard earth, 'guardian of my secrets; O stars who with the golden moon succeed the day; O Hecate, aider of my spells and sorcery; O Earth, source of my powerful herbs; O all you gods of the forest, gods of the night, be by my side! With your help I have made rivers run back to their sources, stilled the ocean's swell, summoned up and scattered the clouds and winds, made mountains to tremble, earth to groan and spirits to rise up from the grave. The moon, too, I have drawn down from the sky and by my potions the light of the sun himself has grown pale. It was you who dulled for me the fiery breath of my father's bulls and yoked them to the plough. You stirred up civil war among the dragon's brood and lulled to sleep the sleepless guardian of the golden fleece. Now, too, I need your magic juices that old Aeson may be restored in years and recover his first youth. You will grant me my prayer, I know it! I can see the stars flickering in reply!'

As she finished, a chariot drawn by winged dragons swept down from heaven. Medea stepped into it and with a gentle touch of the reins she was away, riding on high through the clouds. She alighted on every mountain of Thessaly and there on Ossa and Pelion, and Pindus and Olympus she picked their rarest herbs, plucking some out by the root and cutting others with her curved hook. On the ninth day she returned with her magic plants. Even their scent had such potency that the dragons cast off their old skins for new.

In front of the palace, Medea set up two altars of turf, one on the right to Hecate, one on the left to Youth. Not far away she dug a ditch and filled it with the blood of a black-fleeced sheep. On top of this she poured goblets of wine and goblets of warm milk, chanting her spells all the while and calling upon the spirits of earth and underworld. At last when these spirits had been appeased by the long prayers and mutterings, she commanded that Aeson should be brought out and his body, lulled to sleep by a spell, laid on the strewn herbs. Jason and his servants were told to depart, that the mysteries

might begin unseen. Then Medea circled her altar like one possessed, dipped her torches in the black blood of the ditch and lit them on the two altars. Three times she bathed the old man with flame, with water and with sulphur. Meanwhile her strong potion bubbled and seethed with white foam in the pot: in this she plunged the roots and seeds and flowers she had gathered, adding pebbles from the farthest East and grains of sand washed up by the Ocean's tide. Into the pot, too, went hoar frosts gathered by moonlight, the wings of a screech-owl and the entrails of a werewolf. Scaly-skin of a water-snake, liver of an aged stag, head and beak of a crow, nine generations old—these and a thousand other nameless ingredients were added to the witch's brew, as Medea stirred all the while with a withered olive-branch.

As she mixed the potion in the warm pot, first it turned green and then sprouted leaves, hung with olive-berries. Wherever the liquid boiled over the edge of the pot on to the ground, spring flowers and soft grasses appeared. When she saw this, Medea slit the old man's throat and allowed the tired old blood to drain from his veins before filling them again with her brew of magic juices. As Aeson drank in the new life-blood through his mouth and throat, his beard and hair lost their greyness and became glossy black: no more was he pale and wasted and wrinkled, but his limbs gleamed with muscular strength. He marvelled as forty years fell away and he remembered what it is to feel young and strong again.

But Medea was a wicked woman. Later on, Jason left her and married a new wife. Medea's revenge was terrible. She gave the girl a robe which, as soon as it was put on, destroyed the wearer with its fiery power. Then she killed her own two children whom she had borne to Jason and fled on her winged chariot to Athens. There she was given shelter by the king, but her evil deeds were not at an end. She tried to poison the king's son, Theseus, and the crime was only prevented at the last moment. Her witchcraft brought sorrow where-ever she went.

16. Cephalus and Procris

Like the story of Ceyx and Alcyone this is a story of married love. But the love of Cephalus and Procris is poisoned by suspicion, as first husband and then wife loses faith in the other. We cannot help feeling that Procris acted very generously in forgiving her husband for his cruel behaviour in the first part of the story. As for the second part of the story, the moral is clear: never talk to breezes when you are alone in the woods.

Cephalus, a prince of Thessaly, was married to Procris, the daughter of Erechtheus, king of Athens. The beautiful young pair seemed set for a long life of happiness together. Then one day, two months after the wedding, Cephalus went out very early in the morning to prepare nets for a stag-hunt. His task took him to the top of Mount Hymettus and there he was seen by saffron-robed Aurora, the goddess of the dawn, who had just risen to scatter the shadows of the night. Aurora fell in love with Cephalus at once and carried him off there and then. In spite of the charms of the rosy-lipped goddess, in spite of her power as mistress of the land that lies between night and day, Cephalus could still think of no one, speak of no one but Procris, for it was Procris he loved. He pleaded with the goddess to let him go back to his young wife until at last Aurora had to give in. 'Have your Procris, then,' she exclaimed, 'and stop your complaining, you ungrateful boy. But unless I am mistaken, you will soon wish you had never gone back to her.'

Cephalus set out, then, on the journey home, but as he went he began to turn over in his mind what Aurora had said to him. What if his wife had been unfaithful to him while he was away? He began to grow fearful and jealous in the way that lovers do, and decided that before he revealed himself he would go before his wife in disguise and test her loyalty. The goddess, of course, was only too ready to fan his fears, and aided the plan by changing his appearance. So Cephalus arrived at the city of Athens and went into the palace. Everything was in perfect order. Then he managed by dint of much persuasion to be admitted to Procris' presence. When he saw her, Cephalus' first impulse was to give up his disguise and take her fondly in his arms. She was sad, but beautiful in her sadness as she grieved with longing for her lost husband. But he still kept up his disguise. 'You can have whatever you want,' he said, 'if you will only forget your husband and love me!' But Procris would have nothing to do with the stranger. 'I belong to Cephalus alone,' she declared firmly, 'wherever he may be.' Any other man in his senses would have taken this for a sufficient proof of loyalty, but not Cephalus. He must have further proof still, so intent did he seem on causing himself hurt. At last by the extravagance of his promises he made her waver for a moment, and when he saw her hesitate he revealed his true identity. 'Here is your husband,' he said. 'I have proved you faithless by your own admission.' Procris could find nothing to say. Overcome by silent shame, she ran from her cruel husband, out of the palace towards the mountains, to wander far from all men and their hateful ways.

Left alone by himself, Cephalus felt his love for his wife return more passionately than ever. He sought her out to beg pardon, and confess his wrong. 'If I had been offered such rewards, I too could have given way like that', he said. Procris' injured pride was soothed by his admission. They were reunited, and to celebrate the occasion Procris gave her husband two gifts. One was a hunting-dog, unsurpassed in speed, and the other was a javelin. Each of these gifts has a story attached to it.

The dog's name was Laelaps, and it soon had a chance to prove its mettle. The neighbouring land of Thebes was plagued with a wild beast which destroyed the cattle and terrified the country-people. From all the neighbouring ctities men were called out to hunt down the animal—among them Cephalus. But the beast vaulted with ease over the nets which the huntsmen stretched out in its path. Hounds were unleashed but proved too slow to catch up with the animal. Then everybody shouted for Laelaps, who was already straining at the leash. Cephalus slipped the chain from his neck, and the dog was off out of sight, leaving the huntsmen far behind to follow his tracks in the warm dust. Cephalus climbed a hill overlooking the fields to watch his hound give chase. A strange sight it was, for whenever Laelaps seemed on the point of grasping his prey, the animal just escaped the snap of his jaws, running round and round to evade its pursuer. Cephalus turned aside for a moment to pick up his javelin, fitting his fingers to its thongs, and when he looked up again he could not believe his eyes. There, in the plain beneath, the pursuer and the pursued had turned into two marble statues—frozen for ever in the acts of pursuit and flight. Perhaps some god had been watching them and did not want either of them to win.

That is the story of Laelaps. The javelin has a more tragic history. After they were reunited, Cephalus and Procris lived for many years in perfect happiness, devoted to each other as man and wife. Cephalus still went hunting every day. As the first rays of the sun stole over the mountain tops, he set out into the woods alone with his javelin. Then at midday, weary of the kill, he would make for a shadowy place where a cool breeze blew from the valleys. In the burning heat nothing was more delightful to him than this gentle breeze which wafted from the west—the Zephyr, men call it. 'Come to me, sweet Zephyr', he would sing, 'and blow away the heat that burns me!' Sometimes he would even speak wheedling words, thinking himself all alone in the forest. 'Darling Zephyr', he would say, 'what would I do without you? How refreshing you are to my lips, how I love you!' One day someone overheard these words as he was wandering through the forest, and thought that this Zephyr must be some nymph with whom Cephalus was in love. It was easy to see how his words could be mis-understood. A foolish gossip repeated the rumour to Procris and she,

poor woman, was overcome with wild suspicions. She fainted with
the shock and pined away with jealous fear of her imagined rival
called Zephyr. Yet she could not believe her husband to be faithless.
Perhaps the rumour was false? She refused to condemn him unless
she had the proof of her own eyes.

The next day Cephalus went out as usual as soon as the sun had
risen, and after a successful morning's hunting lay down to rest in the
long, cool grass. 'Come, gentle Zephyr,' he said. 'Come, and soothe
my brow.' Even as she spoke, he thought he heard a gasp quite close
at hand. When he went on nevertheless, 'Come, dearest Zephyr',
there was a rustling of leaves, and thinking that it was a wild animal
he flung his javelin and ran forward, only to find that it was Procris,
hiding in the undergrowth. She groaned as she pulled the javelin from
her body—the javelin she herself had given her husband as a present.
Cephalus took her dear body gently in his arms. She was half-
conscious and covered with blood. He tore away a piece of his own
tunic to bind up her wound and tried to stem the flow of blood. Weak
and dying though she was, Procris still forced herself to speak. 'In the
name of the gods', she gasped, 'in the name of our marriage, I beg
you, Cephalus, do not let Zephyr take my place as your wife when I
die!' At that moment Cephalus realized the whole tragic mistake. He
told his wife the truth, but what good was it to her now? Her lifeblood
and strength were slipping away but as long as she was still conscious

she gazed steadfastly at her husband and her last unhappy breath was breathed upon his lips. There was peace on her face at the end.

Cephalus lived on, and never married again. He still kept the javelin, and everywhere it aroused curiosity, for it was a beautiful weapon, made of rare wood and tipped with gold. Sometimes people would ask him where it came from, and then his eyes would fill with tears as he told them its sad story.

17. Daedalus and Icarus

Man has always been fascinated by the possibility of flight, and this story has caught the imagination of many artists and writers.

Daedalus was the most famous craftsman in Greek legend. Besides building the labyrinth he is said to have made statues that could move. When in our own century the great Irish writer James Joyce wrote his novel *Portrait of the Artist as a Young Man*, which is about a young Irish artist, he called his hero Stephen Dedalus. The scene of Icarus' flight has often been painted, notably by the Flemish artist Peter Brueghel the elder. His picture, which is in the Brussels Museum, is not taken from Icarus' point of view (as Ovid describes it), but from the point of view of the fisherman, the shepherd and the plough-man who work on, seemingly unaware of the drama that is taking place as Icarus falls into the sea.

Daedalus was the greatest craftsman in all Greece. When Minos, the king of Crete, wanted to build a prison for his monstrous bull-son the Minotaur, it was Daedalus who undertook the task and built that great wandering maze that men called the labyrinth. But when the work was finished Minos would not let Daedalus go, and the old craftsman pined away on the island with his little son Icarus, unable to escape by land or sea. At last he had an inspiration. 'Minos may control the sea and the land,' he said to himself, 'but the air is still free. Very well, then—we shall *fly* home.' Straightway he went down to his workshop and there on the bench he laid out a row of feathers, each one next to the other in increasing length, like a set of organ pipes. Then the deft craftsman fastened them securely at the middle and bottom with yellow wax and stout wire, curving them gently to make them like the wing of a real bird. As he worked at the task, standing back every so often to judge the effect of his art, little Icarus played on the floor, chasing the feathers that blew off the workshop bench, or dipping his thumb in the wax and getting in his father's way. Little did he know that the wings he was handling were soon to bring him to his death. At last Daedalus put the finishing touches to the wings and it was time for the test flight. Fitting the wings on his

arms there and then he gently beat the air, and Icarus watched with
wonder as his father rose and hovered, light and free, above the
ground.

All was now set for their departure, but first Daedalus called his
son before him and spoke with solemn warning: 'When we fly, my
son,' he said, 'steer a middle course, not too high—otherwise the sun
will scorch your wings, nor too low—otherwise the water will make
them damp and heavy. I will navigate the journey: you must follow
me and do as I say!' He went on to tell the boy the rules of flight,
fastening the strange wings on to his little shoulders with trembling
fingers, as he spoke. Then when he was ready, after a last embrace,
they both rose gently from the ground, Daedalus leading the ascent,
looking round to encourage the boy like a mother bird leading her
young fledglings on their first flight from the nest. Up and up they
soared, Icarus timid at first, then gaining in confidence as he thrilled

to the freedom of the air and looked down in wonder at the island spreading out below. There was a fisherman plying his rod by the riverside, a farmer leaning on the handle of his plough, a shepherd with his faithful dog—all gazing up in wonder at the soaring pair. And now they had left the coast and were out over the island-studded sparkling sea when Icarus began to grow bold with the gathering joy of flight, dipping and diving with impudent ease. While his father flew steadily on ahead, with beating heart the boy began to mount up and up in the blue expanse of heaven, drawn onwards by the sun's brilliance. But as he approached, the sun began to soften and melt the wax. Icarus scented its sweetness and then suddenly he was beating the air not with wings, for the wings were gone, but with his bare frantic arms which gave him no support. Down, down he fell through the empty air, plummeting in his fall towards the fast approaching sea as he called on his father. Daedalus, turning back on his course, sought his son in vain until, far below, the feathers scattered on the calm sea told him the terrible truth, and he cursed his own craftsmanship that had killed his son.

18. Meleager

The story falls into two parts: the Calydonian boar-hunt, and the account of Althaea's revenge. Ovid is at his most vivid in his description of the hunting expedition. The revenge episode gives him an opportunity to develop one of his favourite themes: the inner conflict of a heroine, torn between two loyalties.

There is no metamorphosis within the story itself, but Ovid adds one afterwards when he describes how Meleager's sisters mourned bitterly for their dead brother and were then turned by Diana into guinea-fowl.

Atalanta reappears in the story of Hippomenes and the foot-race (no. 26).

Meleager was the son of Oeneus, the king of Aetolia, and his wife Althaea. When the boy was born, the three Fates, those sisters who weave the threads of each man's destiny to decide the length of his life, came and placed a log on the fire in the royal palace. Then they made a prophecy. 'Your son', they told Althaea, 'shall live as many years as this log lasts.' When they had gone, Althaea hurriedly took the log off the fire and plunged it into cold water to extinguish the flame. From that day forward the log was kept hidden in a secret place deep within the palace, for the prince's life depended on its safety.

When Meleager had grown to manhood, a terrible disaster fell upon the city of Calydon, the capital of his father's country. The goddess Diana was angry that the king had ignored her in his sacrifices, and so she sent a monstrous boar to ravage the countryside round the city. This boar had fiery, bloodshot eyes and stiff bristles that projected from its neck like pointed spears. It bellowed hoarsely, its flanks dripped hot foam, its teeth were like elephant's tusks, lightning flashed from its jaws and its blasts of breath scorched the leaves round about. It rampaged over the countryside, trampling young shoots and ripe crops and ruining the harvest. Wherever it went it left a trail of havoc, and the ground was littered with torn vines and olive branches. It attacked flocks and herds, and even savage dogs and wild bulls fled before its onslaught. The poor country people had to take refuge inside the walls of the city, not daring to venture out into the fields. At last Meleager collected a band of young heroes from all over Greece to hunt down and destroy the monster. Nearly all the heroes of the time came to his help. Castor and Pollux were there (they had not yet been turned into stars), and Jason, and Prince Theseus of Athens together with his faithful companion Pirithous, and Phoenix (who was later to be the teacher of Achilles), and Nestor, who later fought at Troy, and Laertes, the father of Odysseus. There, too, were Meleager's uncles, Plexippus and Toxeus, the brothers of Queen Althaea. In the midst of all these men (I would never have time to mention them all) was one girl, the beautiful Atalanta. She was dressed quite simply in a hunting tunic, and carried a bow in her left hand: her arrows were in an ivory quiver that hung from her shoulder and rattled as she ran. Meleager had only to look at her to fall in love at once. 'O happy the man who

marries such a girl', he sighed. Yet he was too shy to speak to her, and indeed there was no time, because by now the great hunt was moving off.

The huntsmen entered a thick forest on a hillside overlooking the plain. There some of them stretched out hunting nets ready to catch the boar when it was driven from cover, some unleashed the hounds, while others followed the monster's tracks, eager to trail it to its lair. At last in the middle of the undergrowth they reached a hollow filled with rainwater and covered with reeds and bulrushes. Suddenly there was a stampede as the boar was flushed out of its hiding place and charged its attackers like a streak of lightning. At its onset it flattened the undergrowth and crashed through the trees. The young huntsmen yelled with excitement and held their quivering spears at the ready. On came the boar, scattering the yelping dogs which stood in its way with a sidelong sweep of its tusks. One spear missed and lodged in a tree, another overshot the mark while a third bounced harmlessly off its target because Diana removed its sharp iron tip as it sped through the air. With glittering eyes, and breathing fire, the monster hurtled towards its attackers like a boulder hurled from a catapult at the walls of a besieged city. Two of the huntsmen fell to the ground and only just in time were they dragged to safety by their friends; another tried to escape, but as he ran his knee muscles were slashed from behind and he collapsed helplessly. Nestor would have been killed had he not managed to use his spear as a vaulting pole and spring up on to a branch from which he looked down at the beast pawing the ground beneath. Then Castor and Pollux made a brilliant charge; the boar escaped their spears by retreating into the thick undergrowth, but not before one of Atalanta's arrows had drawn blood, piercing the bristles under its ear. No one, not even the girl herself, was as delighted by her success as Meleager. 'Bravo!' he cried as he drew his comrades' attention to the deed. The young men blushed with shame and urged each other on to greater efforts. They all hurled their spears together in a flurry of excitement but the weapons only got in each other's way and fell harmlessly to the ground. One of the men then swaggered forward with a wild boast: 'Look at me,' he cried, 'and see what a *man's* weapons can do! Not even Diana herself can protect the monster from *my* hand!' With that he lifted his

90

two headed axe in both hands and leaned forward on tip-toe, poised
to strike, but at that moment the boar lunged forward with its tusks
and pierced his loins. The boastful hero fell as his entrails burst upon
the ground with a rush of blood. Then Meleager threw two spears.
One of them missed and stuck fast in the ground, but the other lodged
deep in the boar's back. The monster twisted in agony, dripping blood
and foam. As it writhed about Meleager came up for the kill, plunging
his glittering spear deep into the beast's flanks. A great shout of joy

rose up as his comrades ran forward to shake the victor by the hand; they gazed in awe at the massive beast sprawled in front of them; dead though it was, they did not dare to go too near but blooded the tips of their spears at arm's length.

Meleager planted his foot on the boar's head in triumph and then turned to Atalanta. 'Take these spoils of mine,' he said to her, 'and let me share my glory with you.' With that, he gave her the boar's bristling hide and tusked head. The girl was overjoyed, but Meleager's companions muttered with displeasure and envy. No one was more indignant than the boy's two uncles, Plexippus and Toxeus. 'Put down those spoils, woman!' they cried, waving their arms. 'These things are none of your business. And don't you rely too much on your good looks, because Meleager may not always be there to help you!' Then they snatched the spoils from her. Meleager exploded with anger. 'You thieves!' he shouted. 'Taking what does not belong to you! I'll teach you the difference between threats and deeds!' Then he plunged his sword into Plexippus' breast. Toxeus did not know which way to turn. As he hesitated, Meleager killed him, too, with the sword that was still warm with his brother's blood.

Their sister Althaea, the mother of Meleager, was bringing offerings to the temple in thanksgiving for her son's victory when she suddenly saw the procession carrying the bodies of her two brothers. She shrieked in lamentation and filled the whole city with her cries. When she discovered that her own son was the killer, her grief turned to thoughts of vengeance, and at once she remembered the log that still lay carefully preserved in the depths of the palace. She had it brought out, and then gave orders for a fire to be lit. When the flames were burning steadily, four times she made as if to throw the log on the fire, and four times she drew back. The mother in her was at war with the sister, and the conflict tore her mind apart. At last vengeance for her brothers began to overcome the love she felt for her son and she stood before the funeral altars and prayed to the three Furies, the grim goddesses of vengeance. Then she called upon the spirits of her dead brothers. 'You have won,' she told them, 'and I will avenge you as a sister, provided that I follow you into death—you and the son I must kill for your sakes!' Then turning her head away, with trembling hands she threw the log into the middle of the flames.

As it caught alight, licked by the unwilling flames, it seemed to give a groan.

Meleager was elsewhere, quite unaware of these events. Suddenly he felt his innards being scorched by a hidden flame and it took all his courage to fight down the painful agony. He was dying—but his only grief was that it should be so inglorious a death, far from battle. He called upon his grandfather, his father, brothers and sisters—yes, even upon his mother, they say. As the flames grew, so did his pain, then both died down slowly. When it was over, as the white ash formed on the log's dying embers, the boy's last breath gradually dissolved into air. All Calydon mourned for him, young and old alike. As for his mother, knowing what a terrible deed she had done, she drove a sword through her own body to take vengeance on herself.

19. Philemon and Baucis

The story of the god who comes in disguise to be entertained in a human home is a favourite theme in ancient literature. We have already met it in the story of Lycaon, and there are several examples in the Bible, where Abraham (Genesis 1[18]) and Lot (Genesis 1[19]) give hospitality to guests from heaven. The story of Philemon and Baucis is set in Phrygia (modern Turkey); the worship of Jupiter and Mercury must have been especially strong there because in the Acts of the Apostles (14[11]) we are told that when Paul and Barnabas visited the neighbouring town of Lystra the local inhabitants thought they were the two gods in disguise.

The description of the old couple's cottage is as vivid as a painting. Dryden expressed what many people have felt when he said 'I see Philemon and Baucis as perfectly before me as if some ancient painter had drawn them'. It seems a pity that the gods did not leave the nice old cottage as it was, instead of turning it into a showy golden temple.

If you go to the hills of Phrygia, you may come to a place where a linden tree and an oak grow side by side, surrounded by a low wall. Nearby is a stretch of country which was once good farming land, but now is covered by a marshy lake and echoes to the cries of coots and moorhens. There is a story attached to this place. Once upon a time Jupiter and Mercury came to it in the disguise of mortal men. It was evening and they wanted shelter for the night, but no one would take them in or give them hospitality. They knocked at a hundred doors but everywhere they were turned away, until at last they reached a little thatched cottage, the home of a gentle old pair, Philemon and his wife Baucis. These two had married young and grown old together in their cottage, content with their life of simple poverty. When the visitors entered, bending their heads in the low doorway, Philemon laid out chairs on which Baucis set clean new covers she had woven herself. In the fireplace she fanned the smouldering cinders to flame, feeding them with dry twigs and leaves. Then she gathered fuel, which had been stored in the loft, while her husband went out into the garden to cut a fresh green cabbage. With a long fork she lifted down a side of smoked bacon that had been hanging from the rafters above the fireplace to mature, and cut off a piece to boil in the bubbling pot.

As they worked, the old people entertained their visitors with talk until dinner was ready. Baucis prepared a couch for the meal and brought out her best coverlet which she kept for special occasions and feast days, though it was really old and worn. Then she tucked up her skirts and began to lay the table. Did I say table? Well, it had three legs but one of them was shorter than the rest and a tile had to be found to stop it wobbling. At last the simple feast could be spread. There were grey-green olives and pickled cherries, endives and radishes, cheese and eggs—all served on plates of earthenware. Then goblets were brought, wooden goblets of beechwood, with the inside of the cup lined with wax. This was enough to whet the visitors' appetites, and soon afterwards came the main course, served piping hot from the fire and with vintage wine to wash it down. When this was cleared away, it was time for the dessert: nuts, wrinkled dates, plums, fragrant apples served in baskets, and in the centre of the table a fresh, golden honeycomb. The old people beamed with delight as they served the visitors and sat back to enjoy the company. What a merry meal they made of the simple country fare! The talk flowed as the wine flowed, for there never seemed to be an end of wine. Suddenly the old people realized that every time they emptied the wine jug, it filled again of its own accord. They were struck with fear and wonder and went down on their knees to beg the wonder-working strangers, whoever they might be, to be gentle with them and forgive their poor and hastily prepared meal. Perhaps they should offer a sacrifice to the godlike guests? All they had was one single goose which kept guard over the little house, but when they tried to catch it the goose was too quick for their slow old legs and it ran to the gods for refuge. It was time for Jupiter and Mercury to reveal themselves. 'Yes,' they said, 'we are gods, and we are going to punish the people of this neighbourhood for their wickedness because they would not give us a welcome. You alone will be spared, because you took us into your home and gave us hospitality. Leave your cottage and come with us, up the slopes of that mountain over there.' The good old pair obeyed, and hobbling on their sticks they began to climb the steep slopes.

When they had almost reached the top they turned round to look back. Down there, the whole countryside was covered by the waters of a lake. The only thing that remained was their own little cottage which, as they watched, suddenly began to change into a splendid temple: the wooden posts propping up the roof turned into solid columns, the roof was covered with gold and the floor with marble. As they looked down in amazement Jupiter spoke to them. 'Good Philemon and gentle Baucis,' he said. 'Tell me what is your wish.' Philemon exchanged a few murmured words with his wife before replying. 'All we ask,' he said, 'is to be the priests and guardians of your temple, and as we have lived all these years in loving harmony, do not let either of us outlive the other.'

Their wish was granted. As long as they lived they were the guardians of the temple, and at last when they had come to the end of their years, one day, while they were standing in front of the shrine, each saw the other suddenly begin to sprout leaves, like a tree. As their faces disappeared in the gathering tree-tops, they bade each other their last farewell before the bark closed over their lips. The trees remain to this day and a local guide will point them out to you, the two of them standing side by side in close companionship.

20. Erysichthon

This is really a cautionary tale, warning of the dreadful consequences that follow from not showing proper respect for the gods. The description of Hunger in this story is a good example of the way in which Ovid loves to describe abstract things as if they were real persons (another instance is the description of Sleep in the Ceyx and Alcyone story, No. 29). The whole episode gives Ovid an opportunity to indulge his taste for fanciful and strange contrasts.

Once, in the middle of a forest, lived a man called Erysichthon. On feast days, when the country people brought offerings to lay on the altars of the gods, Erysichthon stayed at home, because he treated the gods with scorn and contempt. He even dared to cut down the trees in the sacred grove of Ceres, the goddess of harvests—an unheard-of crime. In the middle of this grove there was a venerable oak. The local people said it was holy, and hung garlands of flowers on its branches as prayer offerings, and on summer evenings the nymphs danced beneath it in a ring. It was the tallest tree in the whole forest. Yet this did not stop Erysichthon. Breaking into the grove, the wicked man told his servants to cut down the sacred oak, and when he saw them hesitating and hanging back, he snatched up an axe himself. 'It can be a goddess itself, for all I care', he cried. 'Watch me bring it toppling down!' As he raised his axe, ready to swing it with a savage sideways blow, the tree trembled and groaned and its leaves, acorns and branches turned pale with fright. The axe fell, cutting a great gash in the trunk, and the bystanders were amazed to see blood flowing from the wound as freely as from a bull that is killed at the altar for sacrifice. One of the crowd tried to stop Erysichthon from going further with this madness but instead of listening, Erysichthon turned on him: 'Take that for your pains', he cried, and swung the axe at the man's head, lopping it off his body. As he turned back to the tree, redoubling his violent blows, suddenly a voice came out of its inmost depths: 'I who live within this tree am a nymph, beloved by Ceres, and I warn you with my dying breath that you will pay for this deed. I can die happy, now that I know your punishment is near.'

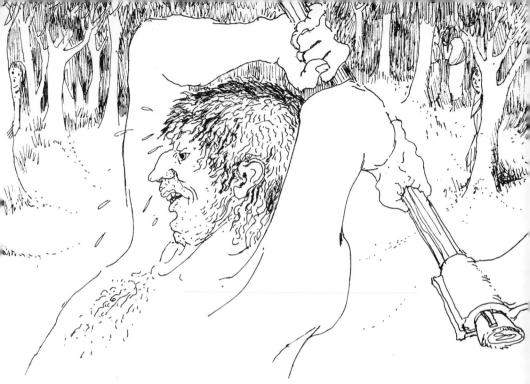

But Erysichthon, deaf to all warnings, pressed on with his wicked work until at last the tree began to sway: ropes were attached to the trunk, and slowly it heeled over and crashed down with a great roar, flattening the undergrowth around. All the other wood-nymphs of the neighbourhood were frightened out of their wits and, dressed in mourning black out of grief for their dead sister, they went to Ceres, and begged her to punish Erysichthon for his deed. The goddess of harvests granted their request and as she nodded her head, her fields of corn, too, waved and the ripe wheat-ears shook on their stalks. They may have been shaking out of fright, because the punishment which Ceres decided upon was terrible indeed. Erysichthon was to die at the torturing hand of Hunger.

Now because Ceres is the goddess of harvest, she is not allowed to come face to face with Hunger, so she sent one of her mountain nymphs, giving her directions for the journey. 'Go to the farthest dark edge of the icy north,' she said, 'until you come to a bleak land where no grass grows. Here you will find gaunt Hunger, with her companions, Cold, Pallor and Trembling. Tell her to take possession of that wicked man and enter his inmost being so that no harvests of mine can ever fill his gnawing need. Off with you now! The journey is long, but here—take my chariot and my dragons to speed you on your way.' The messenger took the reins and drove through the skies until she was over the icy wastes of Scythia. There she brought the dragons to land and went in search of Hunger. She found her in a stony field, frantically tearing at a few blades of grass with her teeth and nails. She was deadly pale and hollow-eyed, with uncombed hair and red sores on her throat. Through her hard, cracked skin you could see the bones sticking out beneath, the bones of a pale and

haggard skeleton. Not daring to get close, the nymph hastily delivered her message from a distance and then, without staying a moment longer than was necessary, and although she had only just arrived, she leapt into the chariot and started on the long journey back as fast as she could go. One glimpse of Hunger was more than enough.

Hunger, meanwhile, lost no time in carrying out Ceres' commands. That night she swooped down on Erysichthon's house and softly entered his bedroom: taking him firmly in her two withered arms she breathed her spirit into his mouth so that it filled his whole body. Then, when her work was done, she hurried back through the air to her cold and lonely home in the north.

Erysichthon was still asleep, but in his sleep he began to dream of a magnificent banquet, and as he dreamt he began to chew and swallow imaginary food. Then he woke up, and at once he was filled with a wild, raging hunger that would not be satisfied. To fill his endlessly aching belly he called for everything he could lay his hands on, all the food that could be got on land or sea or air, and still his belly would not be satisfied, but cried out for more. Food and provisions that would have been more than enough for a whole city could not fill his appetite, and the more he ate the more he hungered still.

Everything Erysichthon had, all his family savings, went to buy food to fill the gaping hole that his hunger made, and soon he had nothing left, save only his daughter—a good girl, who deserved a better father. And now she too was sold as a slave so that Erysichthon could go on eating. The poor girl was bitterly ashamed and ran away from her new master. As he followed in hot pursuit, she came to the sea-shore and held out her hands over the water, pleading for help. Neptune the sea-god heard her cry, and there and then changed her into a fisherman standing quietly on the shore with rod and line. Hardly had this happened when the angry master arrived on the scene and ran up to the fisherman. 'I wish you a calm sea and a good catch, Sir,' he said, 'but please tell me, have you seen a girl, poorly dressed and with her hair all dishevelled? I saw her come this way but her footprints don't go any farther. Which way did she go?' Erysichthon's daughter realized that the god had saved her. 'I am sorry,' she replied, 'but I have been so intent on my fishing that I have had no time to look round. But you can be sure that no one has been on this shore, man or woman—except for me, of course.' The disappointed master had to take her word for it, and walked slowly and sadly homewards, cheated of his prey. The girl became herself again, but when her father discovered her new magic power of changing into different shapes, he sold her again and again to one master after another and every time she would return to him, sometimes as a bird, sometimes as a stag, sometimes as an ox. But even this shameful slave trade did not earn enough money to fill Erysichthon's larder, and at last, when the cupboard was bare and nothing was left to eat he turned his hunger on himself. Yes, the poor man began to tear at his own flesh and the neighbours stood by in horror as he slowly fed himself on himself until at last nothing was left. Erysichthon was all gone.

21. Atalanta

There are many folk-tales which tell of the suitors who try in vain to win the hand of a beautiful but cruel princess. The Greeks, who loved all forms of competition and athletic contest, linked this theme with the description of a running race. Ovid, with his sure understanding of the way a woman's mind works, brilliantly enters into Atalanta's mind as she tries to hide from herself the fact that she has fallen in love with Hippomenes in spite of herself. It is a most convincing piece of psychology.

The nineteenth-century English poet Swinburne wrote a drama modelled on this story called *Atalanta in Calydon*.

Once upon a time, in the land of Calydon, there lived a girl called Atalanta. She was not only beautiful, but she could run faster than anyone else alive. There came a time when Atalanta, like many girls of her age, began to think of marriage, and so she went to ask for advice from the holy oracle. 'You have no need of a husband, Atalanta,' said the oracle; 'steer clear of marriage, for if you do take a husband, he will be the death of you!' Atalanta was terrified by these words of the god, and from that time on she led a lonely life in the wild woods. One day, a group of young suitors came to ask for her hand in marriage, but she would only listen to them on one cruel condition. 'No one will win me,' she declared, 'unless he first beats me in the foot-race. If you still insist, then let us have a running contest. The man who wins shall have me as his bride, but the loser's prize shall be death. Those are my conditions. Do you agree to them?' These were cruel conditions, but Atalanta was so beautiful that all the young suitors agreed without a moment's hesitation.

Now all this had been observed by a young man called Hippomenes who was sitting nearby. He thought that the suitors must be mad to take such risks simply for the sake of a bride. But when Atalanta appeared on the course in her tunic, ready for the race to begin and radiant with beauty, Hippomenes could not take his eyes off her. 'If that is the prize they are running for', he thought, 'then no risk is too great.' He found himself envying the young competitors and secretly hoping that none of them would be fast enough. 'Come on then, Hippomenes', he thought to himself, 'are you going to stay behind

and watch? Try your luck! They say that the gods always help a bold man.' As these thoughts were passing through his mind, the race had already begun and Atalanta sped past to the delight of the crowd: her delicate veil fluttered in the wind, her hair was tossed back and she glowed with the rosy radiance of youth. As Hippomenes marvelled at the sight, Atalanta led the runners into the last lap and over the winning line to receive her prize, the garland of victory. The young men groaned as they faced their fate, but they had agreed to the conditions and so they had to die. Hippomenes, however, was not in the least deterred by their fate but stepped forward boldly and looked Atalanta straight in the eyes. 'That was too easy a victory', he told her. 'If you accept my challenge, you will soon find you have met your match. You need feel no shame at being beaten by a man like me. I come from a noble family and can count the god Neptune himself as one of my ancestors. I am brave, too, so that if you *do* win, you can be proud at having beaten such a worthy rival!' As she looked at the brave young boy and listened to his confident words, Atalanta's heart softened and for the first time she wondered whether it might not be better to lose than win. 'To think of that young boy risking his life to win me as his bride!' she thought. 'I honestly don't think I'm worth so high a prize. It's not his handsome appearance that affects me—though I must admit it *could* affect me—but he is so young. Yes, that's it: it's not *him* that I mind about, it's his youth. I must say he has courage and isn't afraid of death—as you might expect of someone who is descended from Neptune. And he says he is prepared to risk death to win me as his bride. O why doesn't the poor boy go away while there is still time? In courting me he will only come to disaster. There are many other girls who will be only too glad to marry him. But why should I be so concerned for him when I have already sent so many young men to a cruel death?' Atalanta pulled herself together. 'Well,' she went on, 'it's his own look-out. He has seen what happened to all the others, so if he won't take the warning then let him die!' She stopped. 'Did I say "die"? 'Die'—when his only crime is to have fallen in love with me? What a fine victory that will be for me! But it is not my fault. Oh how I wish you would give up the attempt, Hippomenes—or that you were faster, if you must be so mad as to run against me. Why, how young

he looks—his face is almost like that of a girl. O Hippomenes, how I wish you had never set eyes on me. You deserved a better fate than this. In fact if I were luckier, and if the cruel fates did not forbid me to marry, then you would be the one man I could gladly share my life with.' Atalanta's thoughts will tell you more than they told the girl herself. Yes, she was in love for the first time, without knowing or daring to admit it.

Meanwhile the townspeople, led by Atalanta's father, were becoming impatient for the race to begin. Before taking his place on the starting line, Hippomenes went down on his knees and threw himself on the mercy of Venus, the goddess who smiles on all true love. 'Queen Venus,' he prayed, 'be by my side, you made me fall in love—do not forsake me now.' His prayer was wafted through the air by the breezes until it reached the ears of Venus, who was deeply touched by the appeal. At the time she was returning from her shrine on the island of Cyprus, carrying in her hands three golden apples from the magic tree which grows in front of her temple. Now swiftly and invisibly she went up to Hippomenes, gave him these three golden apples and whispered her instructions in his ear.

Hardly was this done when the two runners were down on their marks, the trumpet blew, and they were off, shooting forward on the sanded track as if they were skimming the surface of the waves or racing over fields of white corn. Everyone was cheering for Hippomenes, to give him courage. 'Faster, Hippomenes, faster!' they cried. 'Now's the time to put on the pressure. Come on, you'll win, Hippomenes! Spirit!' The cheers delighted Atalanta almost as much as her rival. Often when she could have left him far behind she slowed down as long as she could, for she could not take her eyes off him. By now his throat was dry and he was panting for breath, though there was still a long way to go, so he took the first of the golden apples which Venus had given him and threw it at the feet of Atalanta. She looked at the gleaming, burnished apple with delighted surprise as it rolled in front of her, and while she turned aside to pick it up, Hippomenes

raced by into the lead while the spectators roared their applause. But Atalanta soon put on a spurt to catch up again. Again she passed, again he threw an apple to delay her and again she went into the lead. By now they were into the last lap. 'Be with me now, kind Venus', Hippomenes prayed, and as he spoke he threw his last gleaming apple in front of Atalanta, so that it rolled away, temptingly, to the side of the course. For a split second she seemed to hesitate, uncertain what to do, till Venus came to the rescue, prompting her to follow and pick it up. It was Venus, too, who made the apple heavier, so that Atalanta slowed down and Hippomenes passed her, flying over the finishing line to win his promised prize. And Atalanta, as you may have guessed, did not really mind losing—in fact as she had to admit, she was rather glad.

In spite of the favour Venus had showed him, Hippomenes expressed no gratitude to her, thoughtless man that he was, and so the goddess of love angrily decided to punish him and his new wife. She caused them to offend the Mother of the Gods who turned them into lions. They live in the forest now, and terrify all who dare to come near them. So Atalanta's marriage was the death of her after all.

22. Orpheus and Eurydice

This is as ancient and profound a story as the myth of Ceres and Proserpine. Though we do not know what Greek music sounded like, we do know that the Greeks loved and reverenced music and venerated the name of Orpheus as the inventor of music and harmony, the man whose song could charm away even the trees and rocks. (We are reminded here of the German story of the Pied Piper of Hamelin.)

Many different nations have preserved the story of the hero who goes down to the underworld to seek his lost wife. The story is even to be found in the ancient Babylonian epic of Gilgamesh. In some versions Orpheus, by the power of his song, succeeds in winning back his Eurydice, but Ovid is following Virgil who tells of the fatal glance back that results in her loss.

Orpheus has come to symbolize the power of music and poetry, and his story has especially appealed to musicians. Monteverdi and Gluck are among many who have written operas on the theme, and the story has been more lightly treated in Offenbach's gay operetta *Orpheus in the Underworld*. The myth has inspired films too, notably the French *Orphée* of Jean Cocteau and the Brazilian *Black Orpheus* where the story is re-told in the colourful setting of a carnival in Rio de Janeiro.

Orpheus was a minstrel, famous for the beauty of his music and poetry, but not so lucky in love. He had not long been married when his wife Eurydice, wandering through the meadows one bright summer afternoon, was bitten by a snake and died. Orpheus was heart-broken at this bitter loss, and decided he would follow her spirit down to the underworld and bring her back to the land of the living. So he set out on his journey until at last he came to the river Styx. Nobody can reach the kingdom of the dead until he has crossed this river, and there is only one man who can take you across, Charon the ferryman. Orpheus paid his fare, and landing safely on the other

side he went straight to the palace of Pluto and Proserpine, the king and queen of the underworld. Standing before their throne, he pleaded boldly for his wife, plucking the strings of his lyre as he spoke. 'Your Majesties,' he said, 'perhaps you may be wondering what a living man is doing down here in the kingdom of the dead. I have not come to see the sights. Nor have I come, like Hercules, to steal your fierce watchdog, three-headed Cerberus. No, it is my wife who brought me here—my young wife who lost her life when she trod on a poisonous snake in the world above. I tried to live without her, to accept her death, but Love would not let me. Love has great power among the living. I don't know whether he ever comes down here, though I should think so, if there is any truth in the story of how you stole your wife from the land of Sicily and brought her down here to be your queen. Let Eurydice return, I beg you. You shall have her back one day, for sooner or later, when death calls, we must all come down to this kingdom, and then you will reign over us for ever. It is not for long that I shall have her. If you cannot grant me just this one favour, then let me die too, for you may be sure that without my wife I no longer want to live!'

As he sang and pleaded to the music of his lyre, all the pale ghosts of the underworld wept for sorrow and pity. Tantalus stopped trying to drink the water which for ever escapes his grasp; Ixion's wheel stood still in wonder; the vultures forgot to peck at Tityus' liver, and Sisyphus sat on his stone to listen. Even the weird Furies, those dreadful goddesses of vengeance, were so moved that for the first time, it is said, they began to shed tears of sorrow. At last Queen Proserpine could no longer bear to refuse what Orpheus asked. It did not take long to find Eurydice, who was among the ghosts newly arrived in the underworld, still limping from that fatal snake-bite. Orpheus could take her back up into the light of day—but on one condition: he must not turn his eyes and look back at her until he had left the valleys of the underworld behind him and reached the top: otherwise all would be lost. Overcome with joy, Orpheus and his wife started up the steep, darkened path, through the black shadows until at last they were within sight of the opening, he in front, she following behind. Now that they had almost reached the surface rim, the loving husband could not afford to lose his wife again. Was she close behind? To make

sure, he glanced back—and at that moment lost her for ever. Down
she fell, down, stretching out her arms to him as she disappeared from
sight into the darkness, grasping vainly at the gathering shadows,
crying a 'Farewell!' that he could no longer hear.

Now Orpheus' grief knew no bounds, and for seven days he wandered up and down the banks of the Styx, begging to be taken across.

But this time the ferryman pushed him aside, and Orpheus was left to his own misery, with nothing to feed on but his tears. At last he went apart, up into the wild mountains of Thrace, to be alone and lament his lost Eurydice. As he sat on a grassy hillock and coaxed a sweet, plaintive melody from his lyre, all the trees of the woodland were charmed by the music's beauty and began to draw closer to the lovely sound: the linden, the beech and the laurel were there, and oaks and poplars and the mountain ash from which men make spears; there were supple hazels, plane-trees, river-haunting willows and lotuses, the ever-green box and the slender tamarisk, the trailing ivy and vines which love to grow on elms, the wild strawberry and the palm tree whose leaves go to make victors' crowns. All these were drawn by the enchantment of Orpheus' song, and when the singer rose and moved on, they followed him, and the wild animals and the rocks followed too, for they could not resist the power of the music,

so sweetly sad. But the women of that wild country were angry because Orpheus rejected them. They went in search of him, intent on having their revenge. Suddenly from a hill-top they spied him singing to his audience. 'There he is—that woman-hater!' one of them cried, her hair flying wildly in the mountain wind, and at that she threw her spear at the minstrel with all her force. But the spear left no mark and when another woman threw a stone, this too, as it flew through the air, was so charmed by the music that it fell at the singer's feet as though asking for forgiveness. This only made the wild women more furious, and now the din of their war-cries, the beat of their drums and their whoops of battle drowned the gentle music that otherwise would have charmed their murderous weapons. An arrow found its mark and Orpheus fell wounded, staining the earth with his red blood. The maddened women first fell upon the birds and beasts and snakes who were Orpheus' audience and then fell upon the minstrel himself like a pack of hunting dogs. Nearby, some brawny labourers working in the fields saw the terrible sight and fled, dropping their spades and hoes and rakes as they ran. The mad women snatched these up and used them to tear the animals apart. Orpheus they kept until last. As he stretched out his hands to beg for mercy, for the first time his sweet voice which had charmed rocks and wild beasts fell on deaf ears as they struck him down.

All nature mourned for Orpheus. The birds, the beasts and the hard stones wept, the trees of the forest shed their leaves, and the rivers rose on the flood of their tears. He, meanwhile, had already started back down that path to the underworld he knew so well. He recognized all those sights he had seen before as he went again in search of his wife through the fields of the blessed dead. At last and for ever they were reunited and now they walk together through the shadows. Sometimes Orpheus lets his wife go first, sometimes he leads the way, and often he looks back at her with loving glance, knowing that he has nothing to fear any more: he cannot lose her now.

23. Midas

This is a cautionary tale, from which each reader can drawn his own moral. Midas is typical of the rather stupid man who cannot appreciate anything but money. We may guess that Ovid did not like such men, of whom there were many in Augustus' Rome, where it was easy to make quick profits. Many of the 'get-rich-quick' men at Rome, like Midas, did not know how to use their wealth wisely, but spent it on vulgar showiness. Midas' punishment in the second part of the tale is well suited to his crime: because he has no ear for music, he is given the ears of the ass—always regarded as the most unmusical of animals. In Grimm's fairy tale it is the ass who judges the singing contest between the nightingale and the cuckoo. Pinocchio, in the Italian tale of that name (made into a film by Walt Disney), grew asses' ears after his visit to the island of pleasure.

Midas, the king of Phrygia, was a kindly man but thick-witted and rather greedy. One day Bacchus, the god of wine, wishing to reward the king for a good service, called him and said, 'Tell me your wish, Midas, and I will grant it.' 'I wish,' replied Midas, his eyes gleaming, 'I wish that everything I touch may be turned to gold.' Bacchus was disappointed that the king had made such a stupid and thoughtless request but, true to his word, he granted the wish. Midas bustled away, delighted with himself, and could not wait until he had put his wonderful new power to the test. He stopped under an oak tree, reached up and broke off—a golden branch! He could scarcely believe his luck. He bent down and touched a stone, a lump of earth,

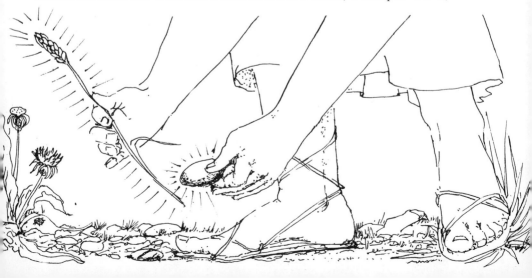

an ear of corn and at once all were turned to pale gold. He could not stop now. A golden chair, a golden table—golden water to wash his hands in—his whole world was being transformed by the same magic touch. In high good humour, he told his servants to spread the tables for a banquet to celebrate his fortune, and sat down to eat his fill. But as he picked up the bread it turned solid, and as his teeth closed on the meat they bit on hard nuggets; the wine he drank down to quench his, thirst turned in his throat into a tawny molten liquid that made him splutter with disgust. Now Midas was filled with panic and cursed the gift which he had craved so much but which now threatened him with hunger and thirst and misery. He lifted his hands to heaven and prayed: 'Forgive me, Father Bacchus', he said. 'I have done wrong, I see it now. Have mercy on me and take away this golden curse.' Bacchus was sorry for the king and took back the gift. 'But your body is still caked in gold,' he said. 'Go to the river at Sardis and follow it upstream until you reach the source. There, in the bubbling spring, plunge in and wash yourself clean of gold and guilt.' Midas did as he was ordered, and the gold from his body was washed into the stream, where you can still find traces of it to this day.

Midas' love of wealth was now turned to hatred and he took to the mountainous countryside haunted by the god Pan, living simply in the woods and caves. But he remained as oafish as ever, and his thick wits were to bring him further trouble still. One day his beloved Pan was on Mount Tmolus, entertaining some nymphs to a few tunes on his reed pipes. Pan was so full of himself that he boasted he was a better musician than the stately Apollo himself. There was nothing for it but to hold a competition between the two, with Tmolus the mountain god as judge, and the nymphs and Midas as audience. The contest was on. Pan was the first to play, and as he heard the whistle of the reedy pipes playing their rustic tune Midas beamed with pleasure, beating time to the simple music with his hands. Next, all eyes were on Apollo as he swept on in a long purple robe, his head crowned with a wreath of laurel, and struck a majestic pose. In his left hand he held his lyre, inlaid with precious stones and ivory, while with his right hand he plucked the strings, producing a harmony of such sweetness and beauty that all acclaimed him the winner—all, that is, except Midas, who had no ear for classical music. When the judge told Pan to concede defeat, Midas argued and protested indignantly and refused to accept the decision. So Apollo decided it was time that Midas had some new ears more suited to his mind—long ears, with hairy bristles inside and floppy at the top, asses' ears. Poor Midas! When he discovered his new ears he was crimson with shame

and tried to cover up the disgrace with a large turban wound round his head. But there was one man from whom he could not hide the secret—his barber. Being an honest man, this barber did not want to give away his master but one day he simply could not keep the secret to himself any longer, so he went off into a field and, kneeling down on the ground, he dug a hole. He cupped his lips to the hole with his hands and whispered 'Midas has asses' ears'. Then covering up the hole again with soil, he went away. All might have been well, but as time went on, the ground where the barber had planted his secret began to sprout rushes. By the next summer the rushes had grown, and as they waved in the gentle breeze they breathed their rustling secret for all to hear. 'Midas-s has-s asses's-s ears-s', they whispered. 'Midas-s has-s asses'-s ears-s'.

24. Ceyx and Alcyone

This story was perhaps invented to explain a belief about the halcyon (or kingfisher). This bird was supposed to build its nest and hatch its young on the waves over a period of fourteen days in winter, during which time the sea remained calm. This is the origin of the term 'halcyon days', meaning a period of calm and happiness.

True or false, the story as told by Ovid beautifully portrays the married love of Ceyx and Alcyone, and the storm scene gives the poet the chance to use his powers of description to the full. The description of the cave of Sleep (who, like Hunger in the Erysichthon story is seen as a real person) has inspired several English poets, notably the Elizabethan Edmund Spenser in his poem *The Faerie Queen*.

Never was there a happier or more united pair than Ceyx, the gentle king of Trachis, and his wife Alcyone. They had not been married very long, however, when their land was attacked by a strange monster, and to discover the reason for this, Ceyx decided to make a pilgrimage by sea to the shrine of Apollo. Apollo, he knew, would make everything plain. But when Alcyone heard her husband was to make a journey by sea she grew pale with fear. 'How can you leave me alone?' she cried. 'You must not make this journey. Only last night in my dreams I saw wrecked timbers floating on the waves and read the names of sailors lost at sea. Not even my father Aeolus, lord of the winds, can help you once the tempest starts—I should know because I saw enough of those winds as a little girl! If you *must* go, then at least take me with you so that if disaster comes we can meet it together.' Ceyx loved his wife dearly but he could not give up his plan now, nor did he want to involve her in any danger. He tried to put her fears at rest, but nothing could persuade her till he swore he would return by the second full moon. So a ship was prepared, but when she saw it launched Alcyone was filled with foreboding and fainted with fear. Ceyx wanted to delay but already the young crew was bending to the oars in steady rhythm and the ship headed out of harbour. As Alcyone regained her senses she could still see her husband waving from the poop-deck. Soon in the fading light she could see only the ship, now on the horizon. When even the sails had disappeared, she returned sadly to the palace, to the empty rooms which reminded her only of her absent and beloved Ceyx.

Meanwhile out at sea, the ship had spread full sail and the rigging creaked as the breeze filled the billowing canvas. All seemed set for a fair voyage but as night approached, the waters began to whiten with the freshening wind. 'Lower the yard,' cried the captain, 'and close reef all sail!' But his words were drowned by the noise of the oncoming storm. There was a roll of thunder and lightning flashed through the murky cloud as the spray flew and the waves heaved the ship upwards, only to suck it down again into the trough. The crew had to do everything at once: draw in the oars, close the hatches, reef the sails and bale out water, while the captain stood helpless against the mighty elements. The waves crashed against the ship's hull like a battering ram smashing at the walls of a besieged city, until at last the timbers began to give way and the waters flooded into the hold like victorious invaders. The sailors screamed aloud in terror, some raising their hands to call upon the gods, others thinking only of their wives and families. There was only one word on Ceyx'

lips, one thought in his mind—Alcyone. At last with an onrush of water the ship foundered and split and as Ceyx, clinging to a timber, drifted into unconsciousness in the dark and roaring confusion, he could only murmur one name: if only the waves could bring his body to Alcyone.

Alcyone, in the dark and empty palace, unaware of the disaster, was counting the nights until her husband's return, busy at her loom weaving new clothes. Each day she went to burn incense at Juno's shrine, praying for Ceyx to be restored to her safe and sound. But Ceyx was dead. How was Juno to let Alcyone know the truth? The goddess sent for her faithful messenger Iris, the lady of the rainbow. 'Off with you, Iris', she said. 'Go now to the drowsy court of Sleep. Tell him to send a phantom to Alcyone, a phantom disguised as her dead husband so that she may know the truth.' So Iris made her way to where Sleep dwells. His dark cavern is wreathed in a mist that no light can penetrate, and only the soft trickle of Lethe's water breaks the stillness. In the centre of the cave Sleep himself lay outstretched on a raised couch, sunk in deep slumber, while around him lay the Dreams, thousands upon thousands in their shadowy throngs. Iris moved between them until she stood before the god. As the brightness from her robes came towards him in the darkness he stirred uneasily and groaned. Slowly he half opened his bleary eyes: he raised his head once, twice, only to let it fall again in weariness. At last, shaking himself free, he heard her message and as she sped away he summoned his son Morpheus, who can take on the shape and face and voice of any man alive or dead, to give him Juno's command.

While his father sank back in deep slumber Morpheus sped away through the night to where Alcyone lay alone, dreaming of her husband. He stood before her bed, in the form of dead Ceyx' drowned ghost. 'Alcyone,' he said, 'your prayers are useless. I am dead, drowned in the sea's tempest as I called upon your name. This is no rumour: I myself bring you these tidings. Let me not go unmourned.' Alcyone with a groan stretched out her arms towards the phantom. 'No, stay!' she cried. Her own cries awoke her from sleep and as the servants ran in with torches she searched the room in vain for her husband she had surely seen. All night she wept and mourned and next morning early went down to the shore looking for the spot from which she had so lately seen Ceyx depart. As she remembered every detail of that farewell scene she saw something far out that the waves were washing towards the beach. It was like a body—it was a body, of some shipwrecked sailor perhaps. 'Poor man!' she thought. 'What a tragedy for his young wife!' Then, as the tide brought it ever nearer she stood rooted to the ground, in growing recognition. At last her grief broke as she cried 'It is he!' and ran out along the harbour mole. As she ran she seemed to take wing and then she was flying and the crowd saw her rising and falling above the waves, a

sea-bird now with plaintive cry. When she reached the lifeless body they seemed to see Ceyx lifting his head from the water in answering recognition. Such love as theirs moved the pity of the gods who changed them both to birds. They are the halcyon birds and even now for seven days in winter, the halcyon days, the winds and sea fall calm while Alcyone nurses her young brood of nestlings on the still waters.

25. Acis and Galatea

Polyphemus the Cyclops first appears in Homer's *Odyssey*, where the wily Odysseus is captured by the monster but outwits him and puts out his eye, escaping from his cave by clinging to the underside of a woolly sheep. Polyphemus later became a figure of fun in Greek literature, and in this story Ovid thoroughly enjoys himself with the exaggerated burlesque. Poor Polyphemus does everything on such a big scale: even his love-song goes on and on. As so often in the *Metamorphoses*, the comedy is in the contrast as the poor love-sick monster goes a-wooing. *Acis and Galatea* is the title of one of Handel's most attractive operas.

You have heard of Polyphemus the Cyclops, the terrible one-eyed monster who lived on the island of Sicily. Long ago, the Cyclops fell in love with a sea-nymph called Galatea. Unfortunately Galatea was in love with someone else, young Acis, himself the son of a nymph. Acis was a handsome boy, only just sixteen, with a faint down just appearing on his cheeks, and he was the pride of his parents' heart. Galatea loved him dearly and followed him everywhere, but the trouble was that wherever Galatea followed Acis, the Cyclops followed Galatea. And Galatea hated the Cyclops almost as much as she loved Acis. As for the Cyclops, that savage and ugly monster was swooning with lovesickness. He really was in a bad way. He forgot all about his flocks of sheep, he left his cave and all he could think of was his appearance. He could do nothing but look at himself in the water for hours on end. The great clumsy creature began to comb his shaggy hair with a rake and to trim his matted beard with a billhook. His murderous thirst for blood and slaughter disappeared

and for the first time ships could sail past his coast without any fears for their safety, since Polyphemus was too busy courting to have time for throwing rocks at them. While in this happy mood, he was visited one day by a prophet, Telemus, who had never yet been proved wrong in any of his forecasts. 'Look out for that one eye of yours in the middle of your forehead', Telemus warned: 'one day Ulysses will take it from you.' Polyphemus only roared with laughter: 'You thick-witted prophet, you are wrong', he said. 'Someone has already caught my eye—and it's a girl.' So Polyphemus rejected the warning. He spent his days pacing along the sea-shore with giant strides or resting his big, weary limbs in the shadows of a cave.

One afternoon he went out on to a grassy hill which juts out into the sea, followed by his fleecy sheep. He laid aside the pine tree he used for a staff—tall enough for a ship's mast—and took up his shepherd's pipe, made of a hundred reeds. He began to play, and the music echoed right over the mountains and the sea. Galatea, who was hiding under a rock in the arms of her beloved Acis, shuddered as the words of the monster's love-song penetrated every nook and cranny of the island. The song went like this: 'O Galatea, whiter than the snowy columbine, statelier than the elder tree, more brilliant than crystal, more skittish than a tender kid, smoother than sea-shells, more delicious than sun in winter or shade in summer, clearer than ice, sweeter than ripe grapes, softer than swan's down and curdled milk, lovelier than a fresh garden—if only you didn't run away from me! Yes, Galatea, for you are more savage than an untamed bull, harder than oak wood, more treacherous than the ocean waves, stonier than rock, more violent than a river torrent, prouder than the peacock, fiercer than fire, more prickly than thorns, more dangerous than a she-bear with her young, deeper than the ocean, more merci-less than a trodden snake, swifter in flight—O how I wish you wouldn't run away from me!—swifter than a stag pursued by hounds, faster than the winds.' Polyphemus paused for breath. 'If only you knew the real me', he went on, 'you wouldn't be running away from me, you would be running after me. Look at what I can offer you, my Galatea. I have a whole mountainside all to myself—a cave cut out of the rock, sheltered from winter cold and summer heat. My trees are loaded with apples, and grapes, golden and purple, are thick on my vines—ready for your delight. This morning with my own hands I picked luscious wild strawberries for you, nestling in the woodland shade. I gathered autumn cherries, too, and plums—succulent black ones and fat yellow ones, the colour of bees' wax. In my home you will never lack for chestnuts or berries: every tree will serve your command! Look at these sheep—they are all mine, some grazing in the valleys, others sheltering in the woods or penned in my caves—so many that I could not even begin to count. Only a poor man counts his flock! You don't believe me? If you came here you could see for yourself, see the ewes, scarcely able to move for the milk in their udders, see the lambs and kids in their warm pens. No shortage of milk for me! Some of it is always set aside for me to drink while the rest is curdled with rennet. You shall have pets too—not common or garden pets that are easy to catch such as a deer or a hare or a goat or a pair of doves or nestlings from the tree-top. No, on the far summit of a mountain I have caught your pets for you—two little woolly bears, so alike that you can scarcely tell them apart. When I found them up there, I said to myself "Those are for my lovely Galatea." O Galatea, lift your radiant head out of the waves now and come: do not reject my gifts! As for my looks, why, I happened to see my reflection recently in the water, and I thought I looked very nice. Look how big I am—bigger than anyone except for that Jupiter up there, whoever he is. See how thickly my hair grows, overshadowing my shoulders as the leaves cover a forest. And what if I am all shaggy and bristly with hairs? Trees have leaves, horses have manes, birds have feathers, sheep have wool, so a man should be proud of being hairy. And what if I only have one eye in the middle of my forehead, gleaming like a great, round, burnished shield? The sun has only one orb and yet it manages to see everything that goes on down here! And besides, think what a father-in-law you will be getting—Neptune, the king of your beloved waves! Only take pity on me, please, and listen to me. See how I come to you on my knees—me, the savage Cyclops! I am ready to defy the gods and all their thunderbolts, but I worship you, my Galatea. I would not mind it so much if you turned everyone away, but you prefer that Acis of yours to my tender embraces. You may fancy him and he may fancy himself but he'll soon see that my size is matched by my strength. I'll rip his innards apart, I'll tear him limb from limb and scatter him over the fields and over your waves—then you can have him all to yourself! My rage is boiling over, heated by a passion that flames all the fiercer for being offended. O how my heart is crushed with a mountain of sorrow, Galatea, and yet it means nothing to you!'

With this last bellowed lament, Polyphemus arose and restlessly roamed through the woods and fields like a mad bull. Acis and Galatea were lying quietly hidden when suddenly they nearly jumped out of their skins as he let out a roar. 'I see you!' he bellowed 'and by the gods this will be the last time you two go courting!' You can

imagine how loud an angry Cyclops can roar when he is provoked—
it was enough to shake Etna through and through. In terror Galatea
dived into the nearest wave while Acis, her hero, simply turned and
ran for his life. 'Help me, Galatea!' he cried. 'Mother! Father! Help
me! You are river gods—for heaven's sake do something!' The Cyclops was already hard on his heels. He wrenched a whole piece out
of the mountain, hurled it, and crushed Acis beneath its weight. But
Galatea with her magic power changed Acis into his parents' shape.
From under the great mound of earth came a dark muddy trickle
which slowly grew stronger and clearer until at last the earth broke
open and a gushing river welled up and gurgled out, lined with tall
rushes. What was even more amazing, suddenly a young man
appeared up to his waist in the stream, with the curving horns of a
river-god on his forehead. It was Acis—bigger, I must admit, and
rather bluish-green in colour—but still Acis, now turned into a
stream. And if you go to Sicily today you will still find the river that
bears his name.

Index